Mum sat [on] the bed and patte[d ...]. It
[...] ince we ha[...] each
[...] he [...] would be [...] around on the
bed and Mum would be tell[ing] me off. Things had
changed. Quietly Mum said, 'Where are you off to, Rell?'

You know something, I really wanted to tell her, but
for the life of me, I couldn't. I don't know why.

'Out.'

Mum took a deep breath.

'Yes, I gathered that you were going out, but where?'

My mouth was dry. 'With a friend.'

'Which one? Priya? Helena? Eh . . .'

'A friend from work.'

Pursing her lips, not in anger but in deep thought,
Mum was trying to be as diplomatic as possible, I could
tell. 'Is there something you want to tell me, Rell?'

We looked at each other, neither trusting ourselves
to talk.

'Listen, Mum, I'm fine. I'm not up to any skulduggery,
like drug-taking or drinking. I'm not sleeping with any
guy, it's just – well, it's just that I'm . . .' I couldn't get the
words out. What was wrong with me?

from The Women's Press

Millie Murray was born in London in 1958. A qualified nurse, she has attended drama college, worked with several black theatre workshops, and been a vocalist in a gospel choir. She created the radio sitcom, *The Airport*; has written for the television series, *The Real McCoy*; and facilitates writing and performance workshops throughout the country.

Millie Murray is the author of the popular Livewire novels *Kiesha* (1988), *Lady A – A Teenage DJ* (1989), and *Cairo Hughes* (1996); as well as *All About Jas*, *Ebony and the Mookatoor Bush* and *Addicted* (with Steve Derbyshire).

Sorrelle
Millie Murray

First published by The Women's Press Ltd, 1998
A member of the Namara Group
34 Great Sutton Street, London EC1V 0DX

Copyright © Millie Murray 1998

The right of Millie Murray to be identified as the author of this work has
been asserted by her in accordance with the Copyright, Designs and
Patents Act 1988.

British Library Cataloguing-in-Publication Data
A catalogue record for this book is available from the British Library.

ISBN 0 7043 4954 X

Typeset in Bembo by FSH Ltd, London
Printed and bound in Great Britain by Cox & Wyman Ltd,
Reading, Berkshire

For Sherelle, Natasha, and
Candice and Annabel Singh

Acknowledgements

Many thanks to Ameeta and Harpreet for all their help.

'A friend loves at all times.'
Proverb 17:17

One

'Let me run it past you one more time, Trenton Bailey, and watch my lips carefully! Right, here goes – I'm not doing it!' I waved my hands in the air to emphasise to my thick-headed brother that I meant business.

'But, Sorrelle, please help us. I know it's such short notice, but please, please, please help us tomorrow.'

Exasperatedly I told him, 'No, no, no.' But when he went down on one knee, clutching my arm, I had to laugh.

'You've got no shame, have you? Look at you, grovelling like a, like a . . .'

'A desperate brother. I haven't got time for shame, Rell.'

I noticed that he'd reverted back to my nickname. I must admit I was beginning to feel a bit sorry for him.

He sensed it. 'All you have to do is sort out the

1

barbecue and a few sandwiches, maybe some pizzas, and, eh . . .'

'Hold on, hold on, I haven't said I would do it yet. Anyway, where did you say Arun lived?'

'Chigwell. You're going to love his house. Every time I go there I don't want to come home.'

Trenton got off his knees and clapped his hands. He knew that he had won me over, there was no more need for him to beg.

'All right then, but I want my money up front, and when I'm ready to come home, you have to drop me.'

Trenton threw his arms around me and hugged me so tight I thought I was going to stop breathing.

'But tell me something, Bro, why are you so eager for me to do the food?' Then, as he started to speak, I cut him short. 'Don't bother, let me guess. Eh . . . Zara, you want to impress her.'

He grinned sheepishly.

'All this for her – you've got it bad, boy.'

'The girl's nice though, she's a peach.' He walked out of my bedroom as though he was walking on air.

Shaking my head, I continued to pack away my study books and sort out my school folders. Trenton was right – Zara was a peach. She was like peaches and cream, with her long blonde hair that she used to entice boys like my brother, flinging it over her shoulder and smiling with her blue eyes that spoke volumes. I couldn't understand how Trenton could date a girl like her. I knew I would never date a white guy. It was a matter of principle with me. Going out with a white guy would just feel wrong, like I was cutting myself off from my background, my friends, everything.

Trenton was taller than my dad, at six foot three. He had shoulders like an ox and skin like a baby's. His IQ could get him into Mensa, no problem, and his looks could get him on the front page of men's *Vogue* magazine (if they had one). His complexion was cinnamon with a dash of chocolate and now that he had a gold tooth, well, if he wasn't my brother I would fancy him myself.

The boy was sweet (not that I would tell him), and he could have his pick of any black girl, yet he went out with a blonde and blue-eyed number. It was a mystery to me.

The black refuse bag was filling up quickly. I was getting bored with this job, but now that school was over, and the exams had finished, I wanted to clear all the junk out of my room as soon as possible. I had made up my mind that I was going to enjoy this summer holiday to the max!

For the last six months I had been working on Saturdays and Wednesday evenings in Sainsbury's, just up the road from my house in Newbury Park. I wanted to work in the Ilford branch, but there were no vacancies. This branch was too close to home, and my mum made the most of it, always asking me to bring home shopping. Worse, when she did her shopping, as she wasn't allowed to come to my till, she'd go to the next one and still conduct a conversation with me. Before I knew it, the person checking out Mum's shopping, plus the people in both our queues, would all be involved in a big piece of chatting about me, schools, children in general, the state of the world, any and everything. By the end of it all I'm

3

sure the whole store knew she was my mum. When she had paid for her shopping someone would always say, 'You and your mum could pass as sisters, or maybe even twins.' I would sort of smile, but really I wanted to shout out, 'I'm fed up of people like you telling me that.'

It was true, though. Mum and I looked near enough identical — though you could tell a mile off that I was the younger one. Also we wore our hair differently — Mum had plaits and I had my hair straightened and gelled into many different styles — that I saw other girls wearing, or that I saw in magazines, or that I just concocted myself. Cocoa butter made our skin glow a deep brown, and we didn't have a spot between us. Whenever my friends moaned about spots and zits I would feel sorry for them, because I never really had that problem. We both had full, juicy lips, and our noses were a bit too big — the nostrils, you could slip a ten pence piece up them, no sweat. But it was our eyes that were the real giveaway. Dad said they were the windows to our soul. Whatever we were feeling inside you could tell by our eyes. Our lips didn't have to move, one look would say it all.

I was happy, in fact out-of-this-world ecstatic, to be black. This may sound conceited, but I don't care because it's true, *I'll say it aloud, cos I'm black and I'm proud*. About two years ago I had made a poster which read 'Black is Beau-ti-ful' and underneath it said 'You had better believe it!' I'd stuck it on the wall at the foot of my bed by the window. Looking at it now, I thought that it needed updating and added it to my mental list of the things that I had to do before I went on holiday.

Just the thought of going on a plane made my toes curl

4

up. My aunt Melda (Mum's sister) was paying for me to visit some of Mum's family in Florida. I had been there with Mum about three years before, but this time I was actually going on my own. In four weeks and six days I would be up, up and away.

My back was aching and I was bored with sorting out my room. I tied a knot in the bag and had just dumped it under my desk when I heard the phone ring. I had a feeling it was for me.

'Rell, the phone!' Trenton shouted up the stairs.

'Coming!'

He must be waiting for Peaches and Cream to phone him. As I picked up the receiver he said, 'Don't be long.'

Not bothering to answer him, I said into the phone, 'Hi, Priya, you coming over?'

I didn't need to ask who was on the other end − I knew instinctively that it was my best friend. What I didn't guess was that she was just outside our front door, on her sister's mobile phone. When she told me, I walked to the door, laughing, and sure enough, there they both were, in her sister's car, laughing at me.

'Well, come in then,' I said into the receiver.

She got out of the car, waved her sister off and began walking up the path. She was slim, with virtually no bust. As soon as she started work, she said, she was going to save up for enormous implants, and she wanted the same stuff implanted into her bottom as it was non-existent at the moment, according to her. I thought she was mad − she looked fine to me − but she said that it was all right for me to talk, I had what she didn't.

'It's in the genes, honey,' I always told her. 'There is no

5

way that I would change myself for love . . . nor money. This package is staying the way it is.'

To me Priya was a beautiful Asian girl. She knew how to wear make-up and clothes that suited her, so what was her problem?

'What you doing tomorrow night?' she asked.

I was just about to say 'Nothing' when I remembered that I had promised to cook for Trenton and his friends.

'Don't say you're busy,' she said. 'Bev's having a party, and we're going. Don't argue, Rell, we are going.'

Priya had made herself comfortable at the breakfast bar in the kitchen, while I poured some Diet Coke into a glass and handed it to her.

I wanted to go to Bev's party, but I wanted to help out Trenton too. This was putting me in one heavy dilemma.

'But I've got . . .'

'We're going, Rell. Watch my lips, you and I are going to have a hot night at Bev's party. That's it.' She got up and began to preen herself in the mirror next to the notice board on the wall.

'But Priya, I promised Trent that I'd cook the food for his mate's barbecue.'

'Not interested, we're going to Bev's.'

At a loss, I sighed, then tried again. 'But he's paying me and I need the money for my holidays. It's for his friend Arun . . .'

Priya stopped what she was doing and turned to me. 'Arun? Arun Basra who lives in a gigantic house in Chigwell?'

I was amazed at her change in attitude.

'I don't know his last name or the size of his house, but

6

he does live in Chigwell.'

'Why didn't you say that? No wonder you don't want to come to Bev's. As a matter of fact, I don't want to go myself now.'

'Why?' I was puzzled.

Priya rolled her eyes as though I was crazy. 'Why? she asks.' Looking me straight in the eye she said, 'He's the hottest guy I know, and many girls, regardless of whether they are Asian, black, white, green, orange, stripes, spots, square or rectangular, are going out of their way to getta hold of him, and you ask me why?' She shook her head.

'So he's that sweet, eh, according to you?' I laughed.

Sipping her Coke, Priya said, 'Sorrelle, I wonder about you sometimes. I know you say you would only date a black guy, but there comes a time in a girl's life when she has to make exceptions. I can't believe you don't know him. The hottest guy in town is a friend of your brother's and you don't know him!'

'Well, I must have seen him around. He can't be that great, otherwise I would have remembered him.'

Priya was right, though. I probably wouldn't have looked twice at Arun because he wasn't black. Well, some people would say he was, of course – that all Asian people are black. But Priya said they ignored the fact that Asian people have their own distinct cultures and I agreed. You should go out with your own people – that was my favourite tune. Black men, like my misguided brother, went out with white girls all the time. They might say that black was beautiful, just like I did, but it was all mouth with them. At the end of the day, if a white girl would go out with them, that meant they had more pulling power and the more their mates would admire them. But what did that say about us black girls? That we weren't as good as white girls, that's what! And black people have to stick up for each other. If we didn't love each other and believe that we were beautiful, who would? All my boyfriends would be black – that was for sure!

I walked to the door and shouted, 'Trenton, come here a minute!'

'What?' he shouted back.

I didn't answer him. I knew he'd come to find out why I wanted him. He always had to know what was going on. Sure enough, he was in the kitchen in seconds.

'Yeah?'

'Trenton, Priya wants to help me with the food on Saturday. Is that okay?'

A smile lit up his face. 'No problem! The more the merrier.'

Turning to face Priya, I held out my hands. 'Your wish has been granted.'

She looked like she had just won the Lottery. 'Thanks a lot, Trenton.'

He screwed his face up, confused. 'Thanks?'

I interrupted quickly. 'Eh, she means thanks for, eh, the Coke.'

He scratched his head. 'Oh, yeah.'

As soon as he went through the door, Priya leapt out of her chair and began to prance around the room.

'Saturday is going to be dark!' (As in wonderful, fantastic, mind-blowing.)

I didn't want to dampen her spirits, but I had to let her

know what was going to be happening. 'We'll be working over a hot fire, doling out the food, so if you're thinking of being the belle of the ball, forget it.'

She shook her head impatiently, 'Oh don't worry, I'll be helping with the food all right. As my mum says, the way to a man's heart is through his stomach.' She stopped still for a moment and I could see her brain whizzing around in her head. 'I wonder if I should make some chapattis and do a curry.'

'Priya, are you joking? I'm the one who's going to get paid here, not you. Don't bother yourself. Anyway, we're only going to be there for a little while, so we can go on to Bev's party afterwards.'

Priya didn't appear to hear me. 'I'm off now.'

'So soon? But you've only just got here!'

'Oh, I'm sorry, Rell, but I've got things to sort out. Look, what time do you want me round here tomorrow?'

Not being sure myself, I couldn't tell her there and then.

'Don't worry. You finish work at 4.45 on Saturdays, isn't it?'

I nodded.

'So, by the time you get home and get yourself sorted it'll be after six?'

I nodded again. I couldn't say anything, because I was so shocked at the way Priya was carrying on. I had never seen her like this before.

'Hmm, 6.30 on the dot I'll be here. Gotta go, Rell!' She kissed me on the cheek and like a puff of wind she was gone. The front door slammed and that was that.

It was amazing. Usually when Priya comes to my

house, she never wants to leave, and she either phones a member of her family to come and get her or she gets a cab. She never legs it up the road if she can help it.

'Hello, darling,' said Mum as I wearily walked through the front door. 'Come and get changed, then you can have something to eat and put your feet up.'

'Sainsbury's was murder today, Mum, and I wish I could put my feet up, but I promised Trenton I'd help him out at his friend's barbecue.'

Not being one to beat around the bush, Mum said, 'Tell him you're not going to do it, you're too tired.'

'I wish I could, but he's paying me.'

'Well, that's different!'

Upstairs in my room I tried to work out what I was going to wear. I decided that as this was work, no different from Sainsbury's, and as I just wasn't in any party mood, it would be my black straight jeans and my bright green top. 'My flat shoes will do,' I said to myself. Flinging off my uniform, I headed for the bathroom. The piercing jets of water coming out of the shower soothed my aching body. I could have stayed under for ages, but I wanted at least a few minutes' rest before I went out again.

Creaming my body with cocoa butter relaxed me a bit. I was just getting into it when the doorbell rang. Glancing at my clock, I saw it was only 5.30. I continued to pamper my skin.

'Sorrelle, it's Priya!' shouted Mum up the stairs.

She was early. I dashed around the room, grabbing my clothes. 'Send her up, Mum.'

I smelt Priya before she came in the door. She was reeking of some expensive perfume I couldn't name. She walked into the middle of the room and twirled around like a model. 'Well?'

She wore a backless, figure-hugging, down-to-the-ankles cream dress, which which left nothing to the imagination.

'Where are you going, Priya?' I asked in amazement, as I stood in my jeans and top, with one shoe on and the other in my hand.

'I'm helping you with the barbecue, remember?'

'Dressed like that? Are you joking?'

She pointed to me. 'Look how *you're* dressed – or are you getting undressed?'

Putting my other shoe on, I said, 'I'm going like this,' then I looked at Priya again. 'You must really have got it bad for this Arun guy to go to all this trouble.'

'I just believe in making the best of yourself.' Priya said coolly, but I could see that she was really excited.

'Well, I hope he notices you.' I knew everyone was going to notice *her*.

'Oh Rell, I can't wait to get there. When I told my mum that I was going to the Basra house she was really pleased.'

'Really?'

'Yeah. The Basra family are very well respected. Not to mention rich!'

'Calm down, girl! You haven't met him yet!'

I had to laugh at Priya. But I hoped she didn't have too high hopes of the night ahead. She might be very disappointed.

I led the way downstairs, and there I had another shock. Priya, or her mother, had made two big pots of curry and a pile of chapattis. I stood looking at it all open-mouthed.

Trenton came in, already dressed in jeans and a shirt. 'You're early, girls. Do you want to go now?'

'Yes,' said Priya before I could get the words out.

He gave Priya a quick look-over, but he didn't comment on her dress. 'What's in the pots?'

'Curry,' said Priya.

Trenton didn't say thanks, or how much do I owe you, or anything, he just picked up the pots one at a time and put them in the boot of the car.

'See you, Mum.'

Mum came out of the kitchen with a tea towel in her hand. ' What about something to eat, Sorrelle?'

'I'll get something at the barbecue, Mum. See you later.' I kissed her on the cheek, and out the door we all went.

Two

Trenton drove as though his shoes were too tight and Priya chatted as though she'd been given the truth drug and was revealing all. I sat quietly in the back feeling bored with them. I began to think of the plane I would be taking to Florida. I could hear the engine roaring as it sped down the runway, lifting off, soaring through the endless clouds until – sunshine, sand and sea and, and . . .

'Snap to it, Rell, we're here,' said Priya.

Trenton was already out of the car, hauling a pot. I surveyed my surroundings quickly. Impressive. Lots and lots of money. The detached house was massive – my house plus five others down my road could have fitted in easily. I wanted to stand and drink it all in, but a guy whose face I sort of remembered came dashing out to us.

'Hi, Trenton, let me give you a hand.'

Priya nearly fainted. I gave her a quick jab in the ribs

and she straightened up.

'Please come in.' Turning to me with a smile he said, 'It's Sorrelle, isn't it?'

Smiling back at him, I nodded.

He didn't seem to acknowledge Priya, so I introduced her, and he smiled at her too.

'Oh Arun, I'm so glad you invited me. I'm really happy to be here. Tonight's going to be great . . .'

Arun smiled vaguely and walked off. This was getting beyond a joke. 'Have a few screws dropped out your head or something, Priya? So you fancy Arun, fine. But play it a *bit* cool!'

'Rell, you don't understand.'

'You're right, I don't!'

The kitchen was about ten miles from the front door. I was worn out by the time we got there, but I didn't even have time to catch my breath. Arun pointed out the fridge, cooker, cutlery drawer, dishwasher and food cupboards, then he led me outside and showed me the barbecue.

'Do you think you'll be all right?'

'Yeah, Priya's come to help me. Priya . . .' I turned round to speak to her, but she wasn't there. Big waves of embarrassment washed over me. I didn't know what to say.

'Oh don't worry about her,' said Arun kindly. 'She's probably gone to the loo or something.'

I mumbled something under my breath.

'Do you want a drink?'

'A cup of tea will be fine.'

'Sit yourself down. I'll make it,' he said. So I did.

Trenton breezed in. 'I'm off to pick up Zara, Rell. Arun, I'll see you later.'

'But Trenton . . .' I was pleading with him with my eyes not to leave me on my own, but he ignored me.

'Later.' He zoomed off.

There was an uncomfortable silence, but it gave me a few minutes to check out my surroundings.

The kitchen was big – there was no other way to describe it – and it contained every mod con imaginable. Arun brought the tea over and sat down facing me.

'Thanks for stepping in at the last minute, and . . .' He slipped his hand in his pocket and pulled out some money. 'Here we go.' He handed me thirty quid.

'Oh, but Trenton said twenty,' I said, stupidly trying to hand back ten.

'No, come on, take it, I want you have it.'

Shrugging my shoulders, I thanked him and put the money in my purse.

He began to talk about his parents being away, and explained that since they would be back soon he thought he might as well have some fun. As he spoke I was able to scrutinise him and see why Priya was making all the fuss. No way was he as good-looking as Trenton, he was just okay. His shoulder-length hair was thick, black and shiny, and he had a hint of a moustache. It was his eyes that I found appealing – not that I fancied him or anything, but they made him seem vulnerable, like a little child. I didn't expect him to be like this, I thought he'd be more flashy and showy and have loads of confidence, but he seemed quite homely and calm. I liked him.

We both looked around the room. I thought he must

be feeling just as awkward as me, because, obviously desperate for something to say, he garbled, 'I've had terrible toothache and I've had to take some antibiotics. Thank goodness, it's almost gone now. It was one of my back teeth – have a look.'

I didn't particularly want to be looking in his mouth, but he leaned over to me, so I had to lean over to him and peer into it. Not knowing what to look for, I made a few noises as if I did. That was when Priya walked in. She stopped and glared at us.

'Oh, Priya,' I said, feeling somehow as if I'd been caught out doing something really bad. 'We were . . .'

Arun chipped in quickly. 'There you are, Priya. We were wondering where you'd got to.' He stood up and said to me, 'When you're ready you can start sorting some of the food out, Rell.' I nodded. My nickname came out of his mouth so naturally, it caught me out.

'C'mon Priya, let's get cracking.'

Reluctantly she began to help me sort through the mountain of food. As soon as Arun had left through the back door, she turned to me.

'What were you up to, Rell?'

'He was showing me his bad tooth, would you believe? More to the point, where have you been? Have you been in this house before?'

'No, but I was dying to go to the loo.'

'Liar, you've been having a nose.'

Then she was off – the house was wonderful, like something she had always dreamed about. It must be heaven living here . . . And wasn't Arun gorgeous – had I noticed his eyes . . . ?

'You don't seem to have made a great impression on him,' I interrupted. 'I couldn't handle someone I hardly know coming into my house and wandering off on their own. I think he's been really good about it. If I were him, I would be dealing with you.' I pointed my finger at her.

'Hmm, maybe he likes me and didn't want to upset me.'

'Dream on.'

The evening flashed by. Glancing at my watch, I was surprised that it was nearly midnight. I had seen Priya wandering about a couple of hours ago with a wine glass in her hand, and as for Trenton, he only turned up when he wanted something to eat. His girlfriend Zara spent all night glued to his arm as though he was her life-line and she wouldn't be able to breathe without him.

As for Arun, sometimes when I glanced up I'd catch him looking at me, and he'd smile quickly then look away. Once or twice he came up to me and asked if I was okay. There was always a girl or two hot on his heels behind him. Priya was right. He seemed to attract any girl. At first I told myself that it was because of his money, or more correctly his parents' money, but then I had to admit that he was actually quite fanciable. In spite of the vulnerable look I'd noticed earlier, he also seemed quite self-assured. It was an attractive combination.

Yawning, I sat at the kitchen table, finding it difficult to keep my eyes open. I rested my head on my arms. The embers from the barbecue had slowly died a cold death. The table of food looked as though an army of locusts had paid it a visit, yet nobody seemed to want to go home.

'Tired?'

Looking up, I saw Arun smiling down at me.

'Worn out and ready for a deep sleep.' I tried to smile back but I yawned instead.

'Would you like to go home now?' he asked.

'Right this very minute, but I can't be bothered to look for Trenton. If you see him around, could you tell him I want to go now?'

Arun put his hand into his pocket and pulled out some keys. 'I'll do one better than that, I'll take you myself.'

My eyes sprang open. 'But I don't want to put you out!'

'Not at all, it'll be my pleasure.'

Images of my lovely bed kept popping up before my eyes like a mirage. I couldn't wait to get home. Then I remembered something.

'What about Priya? How will she get home?'

'Did you call me, Rell?' I don't know where Priya suddenly sprang from, but there she was and I didn't want to waste any time or effort thinking about it.

'C'mon, we're going home.'

'But it's too early, Rell.'

Arun said, 'I'm taking her, Priya, would you like a lift home too?'

His words were barely out of his mouth when Priya replied, 'I'm ready.'

The journey home would have been enjoyable if Priya had stopped yakking like a parrot. I don't know what make the car was, but it was so smooth it reminded me of a jumbo jet.

Eventually we pulled up a few doors away from Priya's house. 'Oh, you've gone past my house,' she said idiotically.

Arun reversed the car.

She climbed out. 'It was a fantastic night, Arun, thanks so much for a lovely time,' she went on.

'Hmm,' was all he said.

'Speak to you tomorrow, Rell, and Arun, if ever you need anyone again to help you with food arrangements, here's my home phone number. Feel free to call me at any time.' She pecked him on the cheek. 'Bye' she called as Arun drove off.

'Is she always so . . . well, so chatty?' Arun asked.

'Well, she's a bit over the top sometimes, but I think she's had one glass too many.' I felt compelled to make an excuse for her. We drove along in silence for a while, and I nearly nodded off, but then he started talking.

'I really do appreciate all your hard work tonight.'

'Oh, that's fine, no problem.'

'Trenton's lucky to have such a helpful sister,' he said.

I was startled. 'What do you mean?'

'Just that he told me the real reason why he asked you to help out with the food.'

'Oh, you mean him wanting to impress Zara! I'm surprised he told you about that!' I laughed. Suddenly I felt very relaxed. We started to chat about Trenton, and then got on to Arun's family, and before I knew it, we had reached my house.

He stopped the car and turned to me. 'Rell, I wonder . . . could I take you out to dinner sometime, to express

19

my gratitude for you helping me out tonight?'

I gulped. We'd got on really well, but I hadn't expected this. 'Why?' was the only word that I could muster.

'I told you why, for helping me to . . .'

'Yeah, but as far as I'm concerned you've already paid me, more than was promised.'

He shrugged his shoulders. 'Okay, it was just a gesture, but if you don't want to come that's all right.'

Straight away, I felt a fool. After all, he had only asked me out for dinner. I'd probably enjoy myself, too. 'No, no, I didn't say that I didn't want to come, it's just . . .'

'Look, Sorrelle, let's say, next Saturday at eight. I'll pick you up and we can go out for a meal somewhere nice. How does that sound?'

I opened the car door and stepped out. 'Okay.' I smiled at him, then turned and walked up the garden path. I knew he was watching me so I took my time, because I knew it would be just like me to rush and trip. Closing the front door behind me, I heard him drive off.

The Cantonese restaurant was half full. There was a table to the right of us made up to seat at least twelve people. We sat at a small table for four, but it was just us two. Arun ordered for us, but I looked at the menu before the waiter took it and the prices were worryingly high.

'What would you like to drink?' Arun asked me.

'Fresh orange juice.'

'That's it?'

I nodded. The waiter took our order and the menus and left.

Sitting back in my chair, I thought about the different

reactions from people when I told them I was going out for dinner with Arun. When I told my mum and dad it just so happened that Mum was moaning at my dad about him not taking her out for a meal as a treat.

'Mum, talking about going out for dinner, Arun's taking me out on Saturday as a way of saying thank you for helping out at his barbecue.'

'Really? That's nice of him.'

'Who is he?' enquired Dad.

'A friend of Trenton's who lives in Chigwell.'

That explanation wasn't enough for Dad. 'Who else is going?'

'Just him and me, Dad.'

'Bertie, drop it now,' said Mum.

'But Donna, Rell is my only girl child and I want to know about any man taking her anywhere. Look how many girls are being abducted and abused and killed by just innocently going out for dinner with their brothers' friends.'

Mum and I both burst out laughing. 'Oh Dad, stop it! Look, you can get his mobile phone number off Trenton, so you'll be able to contact me at any time.'

Dad growled something I couldn't make out.

When I told Trenton, he thought Arun was wasting his money on me.

'You're so feisty, Trenton. He's done more for me than you've ever done for as long as I've known you.'

'But it's the truth. When I think of all those beautiful girls he knows, and he's taking you out! The guy's gone . . .' He pointed to his forehead.

'Just shut up, you!' I was annoyed with him.

I told Priya the next day when she came round.

'He's-taking-you-out-for-a-meal!' she almost shouted at me, pointing her finger in an accusing way in my face.

'Look, Priya. All the guy's doing is taking me out for some food, end of story.' I threw my arms out wide.

'But what about me? You know how much I fancy him!' she wailed.

'What about you? It was me that was slogging my guts out sorting out the food – you were swanning about like royalty,' I retorted.

She stopped for a moment and I could tell she was cooking up something.

'Rell, this is what you do. Call him and tell him that I'll be coming with you on Saturday. That's it, he's obviously forgotten that I was helping you. It's a simple mistake, anyone could make it.'

Puzzled, I said to her, 'What are you talking about? You've lost me.'

Priya then plunged into some convoluted story about why Arun had invited me, and why she should be going as well.

'No,' I said firmly and finally. Priya and I never really fell out, but there were times when I had to put her in her place, like now for instance.

She sussed I wasn't taking any rubbish from her so she changed her tune.

'He doesn't fancy you or anything, so don't get any ideas.'

'I could've told you that. It's no big deal, this dinner date, so calm yourself down.'

Phew!

***

22

'. . . next weekend,' said Arun.

'Pardon?' I had been lost in my thoughts and had not been paying attention to what he was saying.

'I said my parents are back next weekend.'

'Oh, lovely.'

His shiny black hair kept flopping over his forehead. Now he pushed it back and looked at me seriously. It wasn't the vulnerable look I'd noticed at the party, more a sort of searching look. My stomach did a somersault. 'Calm down, Rell!' I told myself, and began chatting on about a film I'd seen the week before. Gradually I relaxed. He was easy to talk to.

Walking around Leicester Square afterwards, I thanked Arun for the meal. I'd had a great evening. The only thing that marred it was the group of young Asian people sitting near us in the restaurant. They kept looking over and they were obviously talking about us. I think Arun knew what they were saying, but being a bit of a gentleman, he didn't tell me a thing. But their body language was giving it all away. I was sure what the main topic on their agenda was — why was a nice Asian boy out with a black girl? One girl in particular was giving me the eyeball, so I eyeballed her back — in fact, I wanted to ask her what her problem was, but I didn't want to drag Arun into any confrontation.

We sat in the car outside my door for a few minutes. Arun turned to face me. 'You know, Rell, there's something . . . different about you.'

'Oh yeah? Different from what?'

'I don't know. From other girls. You seem sort of laid-back. As if you know your own mind.'

I thought of those overdressed, gushing girls who'd been all over him at his party. Maybe he had a point! 'Well, I hope I do,' I told him.

He gave me one of his searching looks. 'Could I see you again, Rell?'

I didn't stop to think. I said yes.

Three

The sun's rays were beating mercilessly down on my head as I sat in Aunt Melda's backyard.

'Yu want some more iced tea, chile?' asked Aunt Melda.

'No thanks, this third cup is just fine.'

Aunt Melda believed that food and drink were the answer to everything. She had tried to shove a plate of pig-tail soup and rice down my throat but I begged off by saying that I'd had a large breakfast, which was stretching the truth, as I'd only had a cup of coffee.

What a way to spend a Monday morning, holed up at my aunt's. My plan had been to have a lie-in and then get up and laze around, but all that got blown out of the window due to Saturday night.

I thought again about what I had said to Arun – I was amazed that I'd agreed to go out with him again and then about the conversation we'd had on the phone on Sunday.

Saturday night was rough. I had tossed and turned in my bed. Why had I told Arun I would see him again? Sunday found me drawing up two lists: one headed 'Yes' and the other 'No'. Normally I reasoned out everything in my head, but this situation was too big for that, so I had to write things down.

The 'Yes' list – reasons why I should go out with Arun – far outnumbered the 'No' list. But the biggest 'No' was the fact that he was Asian. I was strictly a black-man woman. I'd told everyone I knew that black men were beautiful and going out with anyone else would suggest that they weren't. So what in the world was I doing dating an Asian guy?

When Arun had rung me on Sunday I had to tell him that after careful consideration I couldn't see him ever again, and that when I had told him yes on Saturday I wasn't thinking straight, but now I was thinking straight, and the answer was no. Would you believe it, he wouldn't have it. In fact he put me on the spot.

'So why are you saying no now?' he asked me very pointedly.

My tongue got in a knot. 'I, eh, you see . . . Well, it's a bit complicated . . .'

He said it for me. 'It's because I'm Asian, isn't it?'

A long, long silence flowed down the phone line.

'Come on Rell, it is, isn't it?'

Boy, this guy was persistent.

'No, it's not quite like that.'

'What is it then? Unless you tell me why you won't see me again, I won't accept your answer.'

'Our cultures are different.'

26

He laughed. 'I'm not asking you to come and live in India with me, you know.'

I knew that he knew that it was because he was Asian that I wouldn't see him, but for the life of me I couldn't honestly tell him. It sounded stupid even in my head, that's why I couldn't let the words come out of my mouth. How would it sound – 'Eh, sorry Arun, I can't date you because you're Asian. I'm not racist or anything, it's just the way life is.'

'You still haven't said why.' The guy was like a dog with a bone.

'The thing is, Arun, you are used to dating beautiful women, with lovely clothes, who will compliment you as you drive around in your nice motor . . .'

He butted in, 'And who are Asian.' He was so quick.

'Excuse me, Arun, don't put words into my mouth!' I said indignantly.

'But Rell, don't tell me that you really believe what you're saying, because I don't. You are beautiful, I find you very attractive, you have a sense of humour and I'd like to get to know you better.'

My head wanted to say, 'Push off and leave me alone,' but my heart got to my mouth first and I said I'd think about it.

That 'Yes' list was very long.

He was – I had to face it – very attractive. He had nice manners, was quietly confident and had a good sense of humour. He wasn't short of a few bob, and he didn't mind spending it. Lovely car, nice house. All the girls fancied him, and that was just for starters.

Altogether we had spent two hours on the phone. That

had taken three phone calls throughout Sunday. Trenton and my parents thought it was Priya and I didn't tell them otherwise. I wasn't sure what their reaction would be.

Talking about Priya, she had phoned me twice too, and questioned me like an FBI investigator about my dinner date with Arun. I wasn't in the mood for her.

'So did you have lots to eat?'

'Tons.'

'Was it nice?'

'Great.'

'Did you have dessert?'

'No.'

'Why not?'

'I was full.'

'How about coffee?'

'Are you having a laugh, Priya? What is it with you? I've told you a hundred times what we ate, said and did and yet you want me to repeat myself again? Forget it.'

I was ready to bang the phone down when I heard her say, 'Are you going to see him again?'

To be truthful I knew that that was what she really wanted to know all along, and perhaps if she had asked me straight away I might have told her, but all this beating about the bush annoyed me so I told her to mind her own business.

'What do you mean, mind my own business? You're my friend and I've never held back anything from you, so what's your problem?'

That was a lie. There were a few things I could've rattled off to her from the top of my head which she had omitted to tell me, but I let bygones be bygones.

'I've got to go, Priya.' End of phone call.

The conversation with Priya added to my confusion. Why didn't I just tell her? It was hard trying to work it out for myself, adding it all up together and finding that the equation was coming out wrong.

It was in the last conversation that I had with Arun that I finally said yes. I was so worn out that I just gave in.

Aunt Melda's voice penetrated my thoughts.

'So tell me, yu have every ting yu need for de holiday?'

'Nearly.'

'What more yu want?'

'Oh, just bits and pieces.'

'What do yu mean, bits and pieces.'

Not wanting to be rude, I took a deep breath and said the first thing that came into my head – 'A few T-shirts and some shorts.'

'Okay, me will help you out.'

Aunt Melda had been talking all morning until my brain ached and I didn't want to prolong the agony, so I just said thanks.

It was Aunt Melda who was paying for my holiday, after all. She was my mum's eldest sister. She used to be a school teacher at a primary school in Edmonton and was supposed to join her husband, Uncle Norman, in Florida in a house they had bought for their retirement. They had three children – two lived in London and one in Florida. For the past fifteen years, Aunt Melda had been intending to sell up and leave England but she had never made it, she just went to Florida about two or three times a year.

'Sorrelle, let me tell you 'bout married life. It's good when yu live together, but, chile, let me say dis, my marriage has been a lot stronger since we have had a few thousand miles in between us.'

I burst out laughing when she first told me. I couldn't believe it, that she had no plans to live in Florida at all.

"Hmm hmm, my dear. Tek my foolish advice, live yur life first and do all de tings yu want fi do, and then if yu want companionship or picknee, or for whatever reason yu tink it's right time, get married, and not before.'

No way was I telling her that the only reason for coming to see her was that I had planned to meet Arun nearby. I didn't want him to come and pick me up at home and it was too awkward to trot up to his house in Chigwell, and as Aunt Melda lived off Ilford Lane, it was easier to meet him near there. We had arranged to meet up on the corner of Aunt Melda's road at 2 o'clock. The hours had flown by and now I only had about ten minutes to fix myself and get down there.

Kissing Aunt Melda on the cheek, I told her I'd see her next week and off I went.

Each step I took had my stomach muscles going into spasm. I wanted to spend a penny, actually a bit more than that, but it was too late to go back to Aunt Melda's. I'd have to hold it. As I neared the top of the road, I saw him – well, not him actually, his car. It looked very sleek and it stood out from all the other cars nearby. The roof was down and a black guy was leaning on the passenger side talking to him.

'. . . man, it was wicked, you should have been there last night.'

Grinning, Arun answered him, 'I was out of it last night, I was so tired.'

'But next week, you've got to come.'

'Yeah, yeah.'

I stood next to the guy and he looked at me in surprise, which turned to shock as Arun said, 'Hi, Sorrelle, you're on time.' Feeling a bit sick, and not wanting to look at either one of them, I climbed into the car.

'Catch you later, Len.'

'Yeah, man.'

Arun started the car and it leapt into action. I wanted to turn and wave nonchalantly at Len but I couldn't move. Arun kept looking at me, but my eyes were glued straight ahead. I didn't want to look at him. My nerves were jangling, I felt hot and sweaty, my mouth was dry and what with my queasy stomach, I think I was making medical history with my symptoms.

'Is Southend all right with you?' Arun asked.

'Yeah, that's fine.' Anywhere had to be better than Ilford Lane. Every single shop was Asian-owned as far as I knew, and the looks we were getting were not to do with the car. There was open hostility from the Asian girls, in fact from the Asian people and from the black people too. Everyone that registered us seemed to give us a nasty glare. It was very disconcerting. I suppose the Asian girls were thinking just what I had thought. That if Asian men go out with non-Asian girls, what does that mean about them? And the black people were thinking I should be with a black guy. It suddenly occurred to me that it was really rare to see a black person and an Asian person out together.

I wanted to tell Arun to let me out and forget the

whole thing, but I couldn't. We had both agreed to be very frank with each other today, and whatever the result was we would live with it. That was fair enough, I thought. After today, the agony would end, and I would go back to being Trenton's little sister and Arun would be his rich friend.

Aunt Melda's favourite saying came into my mind: 'Man write down, God wipe out.' I have to hold my hand up and admit that I was convinced that after Monday it would be over, and I wouldn't see Arun again. Little did I know that was just the beginning.

Four

'I don't want to go to some restaurant, Arun, the burger bar will do me just fine.'

'The burger bar! Come on, Rell, the food is plastic there. Let's have something decent.'

I started to walk off.

'Where are you going?'

Not bothering to answer him, I continued my march towards the shops. The last time I came to Southend was when I was about six. I didn't know where I was going, but I knew that in the midst of all shopping centres throughout England, there's always a burger bar. Bingo!

Not looking behind me to see if Arun was there, I walked up to the counter. My mum had always told me that whenever a man took a woman out she should always, but always, have her own money.

'Chicken burger, chips and a Coke please.' I pulled out my five pounds. I wasn't quick enough. Arun's arm with a ten pound note attached to the end of it beat me to it.

'Make that a large chicken meal too.'

Turning round to him I said, 'What do you think you're playing at?'

He winked at me and said, 'It's all right, Rell, my treat.'

Pretending to be the offended woman, I said, 'I can pay myself, you know.'

Before he could answer me our meal was served up.

'You can carry the tray,' grinned Arun, walking towards the stairs.

'What!' I shouted, forgetting that I was in public, but by that time he had reached the stairs. There was not much I could do but pick up the tray and follow him.

He had captured a table by the front window. Plonking the tray down in front of him, I sat facing as he tucked into his meal.

'Hmm, excuse me, what's with leaving me to carry the tray?'

He looked up and our eyes met. I couldn't stay angry with him when he looked at me like that. My indignation melted away.

Arun spoke first. 'Eat up, Rell, you know this plastic food gets cold quickly.'

I realised I was staring at him. Bending my head, I forced a few chips into my mouth. By the time I swallowed them I nearly felt myself again.

'You're wrong, the chips are not plastic.'

'Oh yeah?'

'They're cardboard.'

We both laughed.

It was cover for me. There was no escaping it – I was really falling for this guy. And I suspected he felt the same about me, but there was no way I was going to ask him.

'Let's go down to the seafront,' Arun suggested.

'Yeah, why not?' To be honest, I didn't really want to eat any more, I'd only managed a couple of bites of my burger and the chips tasted awful.

As we walked along the pebbly beach, with the sounds of the waves gently lapping to and fro, and the fresh air with its salty tang cleansing my lungs of the normal filth I breathed in London, I felt good.

Good to be by the sea, good to be young, good to be with Arun.

We didn't speak for quite a while. It was nice. But I knew it wouldn't last.

Arun spoke first. 'So what are we going to do?'

I shrugged. My thoughts were all a bit of a jumble.

'Tell me the truth, Rell, it's because I'm Indian, isn't it?'

It sounded so foolish to my ears that I couldn't answer him.

Arun stopped walking.

'Look, Rell, please be truthful with me. Is it that the thought of going out with an Asian man goes against your principles?'

I stopped walking too, but I still couldn't look at him, so I pretended to kick a few pebbles about.

'Okay, if it's any consolation to you, I can't believe that I'm standing here in Southend with some black girl,' and he spat the word 'black' out, which made me straighten up sharply, 'begging her to go out with me. Never in a million years would I have believed that I would be in this position. All my girlfriends have been Indian, except for one who was white, and the less said about her the better. But I really like you and I'd like to get to go out with you.'

This was not going how I'd planned it at all. By now I assumed we would be heading back to Newbury Park and saying our goodbyes. My emotions were in a turmoil. I felt angry, insulted and pleased all at the same time. So Mr Beautiful didn't like the idea of going out with a black girl! Talk about arrogant! But then again, we got on so well together, and I was feeling more and more attracted to him, and he seemed to feel the same way about me . . . I took a deep breath.

'Okay.'

'Okay what?'

'Okay, I'll go out with you. But I don't want to rush into anything serious. Let's just see how it goes, eh?'

'That sounds good to me,' he said.

We continued to walk along the beach. My head was like a Guy Fawkes Night display, with fireworks going off, one after the other. At the moment a Catherine Wheel was spinning out of control.

Not being one to leave things alone, Arun said, 'Was I right?'

Taking another deep breath, I said, 'Yeah,' then it all poured out. I told him that going out with him was so against what I believed that I felt that I was betraying myself and my friends. To think that there were so many young, virile, fit and handsome black guys out there and

36

here I was dating an Asian boy! How was I to face everyone after all I had said? What if some of my friends didn't want to be my friend any more? I remembered Alysha, a sort of friend of mine, who went out with a white guy. Everyone had something to say about it – the boys called her bad names, and we girls were no better. The black guys dated whoever they fancied and nothing was said about them. But we girls always got a harder time.

'Well, now that everything is out in the open, we can get on with having a good time,' Arun said.

'Why not?' I agreed.

The fireworks display in my head stopped, and the cloud of heaviness lifted, but only to just above my head. Somehow I felt that we had come out of the woods but were standing on the perimeter of I don't know what – maybe a tropical jungle. I wanted to be totally free, but I couldn't. These dark thoughts I kept to myself.

We had walked as far as we could and now we turned to head back to the car park.

At first we couldn't agree on where the car was parked, then we saw a group of skinheads a few rows away from us and I knew where the car was. My heart began to thud. Bracing myself for a confrontation, I clenched my fists. I didn't have an umbrella or anything that I could hit out with if need be, but I was ready for whatever lay ahead.

Arun muttered to me, 'Whatever happens, just get into the car, all right?'

'All right.'

I couldn't sense how he was feeling, but my nerves

were jangling. I wasn't sure we'd be able to get near the car, let alone get into it.

As we got closer they lined up to face us. There were about six of them, all with DMs – no doubt with steel caps – jeans and checked shirts.

'Hello, what have we here? A Paki and a Blackie!' said one of them.

Taking a deep breath, I began to push my way through. A couple of guys were sort of trying to stop me, but I looked up into one of their faces, and I thought to myself, 'Yeah, you could beat me to a pulp, but boy, I would go down wringing off your ear and clawing out your eye. Believe!'

I clenched my mouth up tightly, and every fibre of my body was on the alert.

Nasty names were falling off their lips and fouling up the air like dog's muck in the park, but I didn't expect anything else from this crowd. I got to the door and glanced over to Arun. He looked tense.

Another one said, 'Typical, innit? Pakis're not in this country for two minutes and they nick all our dole money, get all our houses, while we have to live in council flats. We have to take public transport, and look at this, look at this mot!' He spat at Arun and it landed at his feet.

Arun and this guy were eyeballing each other and I was expecting any minute now for a fight to break out. The hairs on the back of my neck were raised and I began to sweat profusely. The panic began to rise inside me, but the next thing I knew, Arun had side-stepped the skinhead. I heard the locks click on the car, the lights flashed and before I knew it we were both inside. The skinheads began to beat the car and I saw a knife come out.

'Oh no, he's gonna slash the roof!' I screamed.

Arun turned the ignition key and put his foot down, and the car jumped to life. One guy was standing in front of it, refusing to budge. Arun drove forward and the guy flung himself on the bonnet. His eyes were bulging out of his head with terror. In the end he had to let go. I looked back. I think Arun had driven over his foot. The rest of them were running towards the barrier. My stomach did more somersaults than an Olympic gymnast. The car slowed up as we approached the exit. Arun pushed the ticket into the slot and as the barrier slowly went up the skinheads pounded up behind us. The first one reached the car but couldn't find anything to hold on to, so he spat on the rear windscreen. The roof was still up, luckily. Then the barrier was up and we zoomed out into the road. We didn't speak until we hit the main road. I looked across at Arun. He had beads of sweat all over his face, but his grip was tight on the steering wheel.

'Are you all right?' I asked shakily.

He nodded.

Thinking back to what had happened, I wondered why Arun hadn't said anything to the skinheads. I imagined if it had been Trenton or some of the black guys I knew, there definitely would have been a fight, lots of swearing, maybe even some shedding of blood. I wondered if Arun had been frightened, Okay, he was on his own, but I would have done as much as I could to cause damage and injury.

Hmm. I decided that Arun wasn't made of the same stuff as the knights in shining armour I knew. I wondered how far he would go to defend me. I wanted my man to look after me, certainly not the other way round. But then, I thought, I had got away without a scratch on me. Maybe getting into a fight wouldn't have been the best thing after all.

'Are you all right, Rell?'

'Hmm, okay.'

He squeezed my hand. I really wanted to ask him if he was scared of the skinheads and to talk about how we had handled the situation. But I couldn't bring myself to do it. What if I didn't like what he said? Would I be put off him big time? Why couldn't this have happened before we agreed to go out with each other? It might have helped me to decide whether we were right for each other. Talk about no control over your life!

The roof of the car was down, and the breeze was very cooling. I decided to put the nasty scene out of my mind. Leaning back in the seat, I looked at some of the people in their cars as we whizzed past them.

Green.

Some of them had envy stamped in bold print on their foreheads. I put my arm on the side where the window was wound down, and I thought, this is the life.

Sleep must have overtaken me, because before I knew it we were outside Arun's house.

'This car must be very fast, or I was really tired.'

Grinning, Arun said, 'Both. Come on.' He leapt out of the car and made his way towards the front door with me behind him. He unlocked it and we walked in. The coolness of the house enveloped me.

Looking around, I was impressed. I hadn't really had a chance to take in my surroundings the night of the party – I'd been too busy – but I was determined to put that right now. The hallway could have fitted in at least three-quarters of the downstairs of my house, maybe the whole lot. There were some weird pictures on the wall, and a large vase with some dried flowers in one corner. The hall chandelier was breathtaking. I guessed it must have been made of crystal, and it was huge. They never bought that off a market stall, that's for sure, I told myself.

I was glad that the soles of my shoes were rubber, because the hall was tiled and I didn't like the idea of clomping across this delicate-looking surface.

I made an excuse about using the bathroom and went upstairs for a good nose around. I was getting to be as bad as Priya. But I was glad I'd done it because the bathroom was a living magazine. The suite was cream and black, with shots of gold running through. There were steps down to the bath, and some sort of fine material was suspended from the ceiling and held back against the wall by gold-looking ropes. There was a separate shower unit, with frosted glass doors. I sat on the steps and thought. This relationship with Arun was different from any that I had had before. I wasn't too sure if I wanted it. I didn't know what to do. The minutes ticked past as I sat there wondering.

'How you doing, Rell?' Arun shouted up the stairs.

I jumped up quickly. 'Fine.' I made up my mind to stop thinking negatively about this relationship, and just try and enjoy it for what it was.

I quickly washed my face then dried it on a thick, soft towel and went downstairs. Arun had made a salad for us. It was fancy. He had changed and was wearing a long shirt over baggy trousers. He looked *very* tasty!

After we wolfed down the food, we went and sat in the living room, or should I say a living room, because in a house this size there were sure to be more than one.

Arun sat cross-legged, on the cream-coloured settee, and began to crack some pistachio nuts.

Sitting at the other end of the settee, I watched him.

'So what do you want to know about me?'

Laughing, I said, 'Nothing.'

'Come on, Rell, you must want to know something. I want to know about you.'

'Like what?'

'Well, what you like doing, what you want to be, you know, stuff like that.'

So I told him. I think he was impressed when he heard that I wanted to do something in science, because he wanted to be a doctor.

Then he told me about himself.

'My parents are from Uganda. They had to leave because Idi Amin kicked them out. They came to England with just the clothes on their backs, and friends put them up in east London. My family were quite wealthy and had had land and houses and servants in Kampala. All that had to be left behind – it was so heartbreaking for them. When they came here my dad had to take work in a factory, and so did my eldest brother, Sunil, and my mum took in sewing. My other brother, Harjinder, was still at school, and I wasn't born yet. My dad used his head and soon picked up on business practices here and between them they started up their own business. And now we own wholesalers, factories and shops, and property – you know, different things.' He wasn't boasting when he said this, just straight up, like this is how things are.

'So, after all that, your family aren't too hot on black people then?'

He shrugged. 'How would you feel if you lost everything you worked hard for?'

I had to admit that I wouldn't be over the moon, but I had to say it, 'The thing is, Arun, Uganda belongs to black people, and from what I heard, the Indians were taking over, so they get upset. Anyway, hasn't it all changed there now?'

He was silent for a while, then he said, 'But Rell, that doesn't change what happened to us. And take those skinheads today. What if they had overpowered us and taken the car and left us stranded – how would you have felt? The car was bought with hard-earned cash, it wasn't nicked or anything like that, and then some creep comes along and says, "I don't like the colour of your skin, I don't like the fact that you're on my territory, hand over all you've got to me and get out."'

Put like that, what could I say?

'Yeah, I understand, but black people have had it rough and . . .'

'So you think we Indians have had it cushy, do you? We've been oppressed, suppressed, depressed and every other pressed. Believe me, Rell. Anyway,' he paused, 'we'll show everyone that blacks and Asians can live together in peace and harmony.'

He shuffled up towards me and I couldn't move. I knew what was coming.

It came.

He kissed me and my mind went blank. I'd save the analysis for later. There and then, the touch of his gentle mouth on mine just felt right and I knew our relationship was on.

Five

'Sor–rell–e!' The bellowing voice caught the attention of everyone in Sainsbury's.

Nearly jumping out of my skin, I turned away from the customer whose groceries I was checking out. I knew who it was.

'Is it true?' She was virtually standing on top of me, yet she still sounded like a foghorn.

'Priya!' I hissed. 'Why are you screaming my name out like that?'

'Well? I want to know!'

Instantly I knew what she was talking about, but there was no chance of discussing anything with her while I was at work.

She wasn't having any of my 'I'll talk to you later' chat, she wanted to know now! Insistently she said, 'How long have you been dating Arun?'

That did it.

Standing up, I excused myself to the customer then turned round and leaned over the counter towards Priya. 'Listen, honey, if you don't dig up now, I can see you and I falling out in a big way.' My lips were quavering, and I could feel small tremors up and down my arms. I was angry.

Locking eyeballs with me made Priya realise that I wasn't joking.

'I'll see you after work,' she said, tight-lipped. She spun round and walked off.

My supervisor, Sheila, walked up to me about the same time.

'Are you all right, Sorrelle?' She looked confused.

'Yeah . . . erm . . . sorry.' What else could I say?

'Hmm.' She smiled apologetically at the customer I was serving, then wandered off.

Switching back to autopilot, I resumed checking out.

I must have been so absorbed in my thoughts I didn't even realise it was teatime. I would have been quite content to work through, but Irene – a woman who was a part-timer like me and who worked the same shift – came to get me.

'C'mon, Sorrelle, teatime will be over if you don't get a move on.'

The staff room was a trek and a half away from the shop floor. I don't know why they didn't provide transport to take us to and fro, it would knock minutes off the time it took to walk.

Irene plonked herself down next to me, nearly dousing me with her hot black coffee.

46

'So c'mon, love, what's going on?'

For a moment I stared at Irene's dyed blonde hair, and into her green eyes, my mind was blank.

'What are you talking about?'

'You had a row with some girl, didn't yer?'

My mind was racing. Irene's checkout was about ten rows up from mine. How did she know?

She nudged me. 'You can't have any secrets in this place. I knew you were having a spot of bother with that Indian girl, so what was it? Man trouble?'

Irene had caught me on the hop. I wasn't the sort of person to talk out my business, but the next thing I knew I was telling her what had happened. I suppose her being in her late thirties might have had something to do with it, but after I'd told her I wished I hadn't.

'Well love, I can understand your predicament, but the thing is, what I think – and my Terry thinks just the same way – to save a lot of aggravation in this life, it's better if everyone sticks to their own race. This is what causes wars . . .'

'What?' was all I could say.

'. . . I can understand your mate being upset. Look!' she said, pointing her finger at me as though she knew the answer to every question put to her. 'The best thing all round is that you tell this Indian chap that you've had a rethink and you're calling the whole thing off, race mixing is not right and it's more trouble than it's worth. Then go and make it up with your friend and tell her she can have him. They are both the same, they will understand each other, and you, my love, can then cheer yourself up and find a nice black man to bring the smile back to your face!'

I looked at Irene as if she had turned into a prehistoric monster. 'You're talking a load of nonsense, Irene.' This was the mildest thing I could manage under the circumstances.

Glancing at my watch, I was very happy to see that teatime was over. I placed my can of drink down and got up. I wanted to get away from Irene quickly. She was soon up and walking beside me. 'Have I upset you or something, Sorrelle? I'm sorry, but you did ask me what I felt.'

Who asked her anything? I thought. I didn't bother answering her, it wasn't worth it and I didn't fancy having a row. Besides, I could see where she was coming from. She may be *saying* that I'd be happier with a black guy and Arun would be better off dating an Asian girl, but what she's *thinking* is that she wants whites to stick with whites, not pollute themselves with black people! I certainly wasn't going to discuss this with her!

The time flew by like the wind that precedes a storm. I didn't want to face Priya after work, but knowing her, she would be waiting outside, good and mad.

I was right.

She fell into step alongside me.

'So?' she enquired.

'So what?'

'Look, Rell, I don't want us to fall out over this, but why didn't you tell me?'

Shrugging my shoulders, I said, 'I don't know.'

'What do you mean, you don't know? You must know! We are friends and we tell each other everything, so why have you been skulking around and avoiding me? Tell me, Rell!'

Her voice shook slightly. I felt a bit choked myself. I went to put my arm around her, but she knocked it away.

'Don't think you can soft-soap me, Rell! I'm waiting for an explanation from you.'

We had reached the main road by now and I could sense my temper rising up in me like a launch rocket. Priya should star in a soap opera. The way her nose was flaring and her lips were contorted, she would have a starring role.

Controlling my voice, I said to her, 'Priya, I wanted to give it time before I said anything to anyone . . .'

Pointing to herself, she said, 'But I'm not anyone, Rell, I'm your good friend who's been everywhere with you, and we're like sisters. So why did you hold out on me about this?' Her voice was raised by now.

I raised my own voice. 'Hold on one second here, Priya. Yes, you are my friend and yes, we do share most things, but you have to understand and respect my decisions about what I decide to tell you and when.'

This obviously wasn't good enough for her.

'What do you mean, when you decide to tell me? I don't hear from you in ages. What am I supposed to think but that my best friend has dropped me to date some guy . . .'

'That you fancy,' I finished the line for her.

'Yeah, that's it in a nutshell!' she shouted.

I was shocked. Never had I seen Priya this upset.

Calming down a bit, she said, 'You knew I liked him, Rell. Why did you pretend not to like him, when all the time you must have fancied him rotten?'

'That's not true! I didn't fancy him or have any kind of thought like that about him. In fact, the truth is he fancied me.'

Priya rolled her eyes and turned away from me. 'You expect me to believe that? From the first time you saw him you thought to yourself, I'm going to have him, and you snatched him right from under my nose.'

I looked at Priya sadly. 'Priya, this is Rell you're talking to, not some girl from down the road you've only just been introduced to. I wasn't looking for a boyfriend and I certainly wasn't trying to snatch him from you when he asked me out.'

Turning her head to one side, Priya said, 'He asked you out?'

'Priya, am I a monster or something? Why shouldn't he ask me out?'

'Have you slept with him?'

'I don't believe I'm hearing this!'

'Well, have you?'

'Of course not!'

'When did you start going out with him?'

'Eh, not too long ago. Look, Priya, I've had a trying day at work, and standing in the street getting all worked up is making me feel worse. Come back to my house and I'll give a blow-by-blow account of what's been going on between Arun and me.'

She made a big thing about looking at her watch, as though she really had to think about it. At least she seemed to have calmed down. Perhaps she felt better now that she'd had her say. She looked up and down the dual carriageway as though her personal chauffeur in a limousine was gonna pull up any moment now and whisk her away, then she said, 'No, Rell, I've got things to do.' She gave me a weak smile and walked off towards the station, in search of a cab, no doubt.

I was glad that she didn't want to come home with me. As it was, by the time I'd showered and changed, it was time to meet up with Arun. It would have been more than awkward trying to get ready with Priya looking on.

Sitting on the floor, leaning back against the settee with my legs stretched out in front of me, and my head in between Arun's legs as he gently massaged my head and neck, I told him what had happened between Priya and me.

'To be truthful, Rell, I wasn't too taken with her in the first place. I wondered if she sort of liked me and I could see that if I got into any conversation with her she might misconstrue what I said.'

'Yeah, I know what you mean.'

We were in Arun's cousin's flat in Barkingside, which was between Chigwell and Newbury Park – very convenient. We still hadn't told either of our parents about our relationship, but I felt that the time would soon come when I would at least tell Mum. She was giving me some strange looks and the longer I took to tell her, the worse it was beginning to make me feel. Of course she knew about our first date, when he'd taken me out as a thank you for helping at his barbecue, but I hadn't said anything about him since then. Now she'd obviously guessed something was going on. I just didn't know if she'd put two and two together and realised who it was going on with. I didn't think she'd object to Arun himself. It was more that she wouldn't like me being secretive about it.

'I'm going to have to tell my mum about us soon.' The words just came out of my mouth.

Arun didn't speak at first, then he said, 'If you feel that's right, that's fine.'

'When are you going to tell your parents?' They had been home now for a few days. Again he paused, and then said, 'I don't know. The thing is, we don't know what's going to happen from one minute to the next, do we?'

'True, but . . .'

'No buts, let's just say that when the time is right, I'll be letting them know what they need to know. How will you feel about Trenton knowing?'

'How would you feel? He's your friend.'

'Oh, but he's your brother and you have to live with him.'

'Don't I know it.'

I thought about what Trenton might feel. It was one thing him going out with a white girl, but he might still want me to stick to black men. Just thinking about it made me cross. Also, Arun was his friend. He'd be angry that we'd got together and kept it quiet from him. At the end of the day, though, he was quite easygoing.

'Once he's got over the shock,' I said, 'I think he'll be all right.'

'Yeah, I think he'll be all right too.'

Which was more than I could say for how I felt when I first met Amarjit Kapoor, Arun's cousin. If I had to sum him up in one word, it would be FLASH, strapped across his forehead in neon lights. The funny thing was, him and Arun were like chalk and cheese but they seemed to get on so well.

He was shorter than Arun, with his hair parted in the centre; and he smoked like a chemical factory belching out poisonous fumes and drank like a fish. On top of smelling like a pub, he somehow had got it into his head that he was every girl's fantasy come true – nightmare, more like!

Apparently he had lost both his parents in a car crash in India and he lived by himself, but he was very close to Arun and his family. He really thought he was hotter than chilli peppers, and every time I had seen him he had a different girl in tow! One thing I definitely didn't like about Amarjit was the way he insinuated that I was Arun's bit of fluff.

Even this evening he said to Arun in front of me, before he left for a night on the razzle, 'The bed's got clean sheets on and you know where the towels are – help yourself.' When I heard his engine start up I had to tell Arun about him.

'Arun, I don't like the way your cousin talks about us. It makes me feel cheap. I don't know or want to know what you and him have got up to in the past, but please explain to him, this is a different relationship. I don't even think he could understand.'

'I haven't got to explain anything to him, but I will tell him to stop making nasty innuendoes.'

'Please.'

I was glad we'd sorted that one out! Now Arun interrupted my thoughts.

'Hey, Rell, do you want to see an Indian film?'

'But I won't be able to understand it.'

He stood up and looked down at me. 'You will understand it, I'll translate it for you.'

As Arun sorted the video out, I sat on the settee and thought about how comfortable I felt with him now, even though his world was so different from mine. I looked around me at the flat. Money hadn't been spared in doing it up – put it this way, the furnishers were not from MFI. Arun had told me that Amarjit had inherited money when his parents died, as well as the property and business which had been managed by Arun's dad.

The film was a love story. This man loved a woman, but for some reason their parents didn't get on – I think they were rivals in business – anyway, they both used to meet on the quiet. To make matters worse, her father had sorted out another guy for her who she wasn't interested in. It was a regular Romeo and Juliet thing. There was loads of singing and dancing, crying and arguing going on. All this was being explained to me by Arun as I tried to follow the action. To me it seemed badly made and totally unbelievable, but just when I was thinking of a polite way to tell Arun I had had enough, he suddenly burst into song along with the film.

. . . *Soniya, Soniya, tu ajaa* . . .

I stared at him in amazement. I think my mouth had probably dropped open. Talk about embarrassing! Then he translated the words for me.

Oh my sweetheart, my beauty, dear beauty,
Come dance with me.

He stood up, gently pulling me with him. The song was slow and haunting, and Arun held me tight in his arms, still singing softly to me. I didn't feel embarrassed any more. In fact it seemed quite romantic. Funny thoughts were running through my head, like, 'I wonder if Mum and Dad had romantic evenings like this together?' I certainly couldn't see Aunt Melda and Uncle Norman like this!

Arun was something else. I had dated a few guys, but he was completely different to anything I had experienced myself or to what any of my friends had either. I mean, singing love songs to me! I had to pinch myself to make sure this was really happening.

The song ended and Arun disappeared. He returned with two bowls of ice cream. 'Thought you might like some of this. It's just right for the evening.'

He was right, it was gorgeous. 'What flavour is it?'

'Pistachio nuts and coconut.'

At each mouthful I was murmuring and ohhhing and ahhhing.

Arun ate his with a big grin on his face. 'I'm glad you like it.'

Sipping my mineral water, I caught Arun staring at me. I felt embarrassed again.

'What are you looking at?'

'You,' he said softly.

I tried to get a grip on myself.

'Is there something in this drink?'

Laughing, Arun said, 'Why, are you feeling light-headed?'

Nodding, I said I was.

He picked up my glass and threw the contents in the sink, then he opened the bottle and poured me another one and topped up his own glass.

'I can assure you that it's nothing but water in this bottle. I wouldn't drug you up, Rell. What would be the point — to get you into bed? When that happens it will be something that we both want. No, I was just looking at you and thinking that I really like you a lot. I know it's early days yet, but I was wondering where this is all going to lead. Will it all just fizzle out and we end up becoming good friends, or will we hate each other, or . . .'

'Or what?'

'That's just it, or what?'

That night sleep eluded me. It was so hard to get Arun and our relationship out of my mind. I still wasn't feeling a hundred per cent about it, yet somehow it all seemed so right. Perhaps I should just try and keep an open mind and let the relationship run its natural course.

Priya's face popped into my mind, and I knew that sleep would be a long time coming. What was I going to do about her? I still wanted to be her friend, even though I knew that my going out with Arun was doing her up, but it was something that she was just going to have to deal with. It's all part of life, I reasoned to myself.

Just before sleep crept over me like a heavy blanket, I thought back to Irene's tirade. It made me realise how far I had come. Not too long ago I would have probably agreed that I should stick to relationships with black guys. But that scene with the skinheads had brought home to me not what was different about Arun and me, but what we had in common. We both knew what it felt like to be abused for the colour of our skin. Surely that should bring us closer together? People like Irene had got it all wrong.

Sleep captured me at last and dreams of Arun dominated what was left of the night.

Six

'Don't worry about it, Priya, it's just one of those things.'

'But I was out of order, Rell.'

Grinning, I said, 'Yeah, don't I know it.'

With her head hanging down and her hair falling over her face, Priya looked a picture of dejection.

We were sitting in Moben's, a fantastically cheap restaurant, well, a cafe really, in Ilford Lane. The food was out of this world and the portions that they gave you meant that you didn't have to eat for a few days.

'I suppose you guessed it was the "green-eyed monster" rearing its ugly head,' Priya confessed.

'Yessss!'

'And to be truthful, I still feel a bit jealous of you. I mean, how did you manage to pull it off? The boy could have a stack of girls, one on top of the other, and he picked you.'

'Don't be feisty, Priya! You make it seem like I've got some big problems, or Arun's got bad eyesight or something.'

She mumbled a few words that I couldn't quite catch.

'Sorry, run that by me again?'

'Nothing,'

'No, c'mon, this meeting is supposed to be about getting things off our chest, and clearing the air. What did you say?'

'I said it must be love.'

I couldn't believe that's what she had said, but I let it go.

'Oh, definitely, love at first sight!'

We both laughed.

'I'm glad we've got that out of the way. Now we can carry on being friends.'

'I'm glad too.'

Tucking into our curry and nan bread, I told Priya all about Amarjit. I was somewhat cautious about telling her about Arun and me, so I tried to skirt around the subject. The thing was, I hadn't told anyone about our relationship and it was burning a hole in my mouth. In the end, it seemed, I had talked about Arun for ever.

'Can we have some more water please?' Priya held out our water jug, which was virtually empty, towards the guy behind the counter.

'C'mon girls, do us a favour and bring it here.'

Priya got up and handed him the jug. 'Do you want me to start sweeping up as well?'

'Full of cheek you are, but hold on, I'll get you a broom.' He winked at me over Priya's shoulder.

By the time Priya sat down again I was feeling all talked out.

'Do you fancy some ice cream? What about the one with pistachio nuts in?'

'No thank you.'

'What's the matter now?'

Shaking my head I said, 'Nothing.'

'Too right there's nothing! If I was in your position I would have a permanent smile stretched right across my face. You would think I had had it painted on.'

What could I do but smile at that?

We had had our meal and had made up, and now Priya wanted me to go to the Exchange shopping mall in Ilford with her. I didn't want to go, but just to prove to Priya that I had forgiven her I said I would come. I did still need a few things for my holiday. The trouble was, I didn't feel like going to Florida any more. I'd had this thought ever since my first big date with Arun – the one when we'd started at the burger bar and ended up at his parents' house – and it had got stronger the more time I spent with him. I didn't want to go away when my relationship with him was just starting, and it was all so exciting and new.

As we strolled into shop after shop, Priya's incessant chatting just wafted over my head.

'. . . So are you going then?'

Bouncing back down to earth, or River Island to be more precise, I didn't know what Priya was talking about.

'Going where?'

Holding up a skimpy dress against herself, Priya said, 'Arun's cousin's wedding. Believe me, Rell, it's going to be the wedding of the year. It's going to be big, take it from me.'

This piece of information threw me. Arun hadn't mentioned anything of the sort. Maybe Priya was still feeling angry about me and Arun and was making more of this wedding than it really warranted. Still, I was surprised not to have heard about a wedding in his family.

'Hmm, I don't remember him mentioning a wedding. Then again, he might have, but I didn't take any notice of it.'

'If I were you I would ask him. My family have been invited. In fact, my parents are going to a do that Arun's cousin Sukhi's parents have organised in some hotel in the West End tonight. It's exciting.' She carried on browsing among the clothes.

She had got me, but I didn't want her to know that she had.

I followed her, pretending to look at the clothes as well. Lying through my teeth, I said, 'I don't think I'd want to go to be truthful.'

Over her shoulder she said, 'You don't want to go! Don't be stupid, Rell! The wedding reception is going to be held in that big place in Docklands – only the mega-rich, like royalty and film stars, can afford to hire it out. I tell you, wild horses tied to my ankles and whipped to a frenzy couldn't keep me away!'

'Really?'

I was hooked, but no way did I want Priya to know that. As soon as I see Arun I'll have to ask him all about it, I thought. I must admit, though, I didn't like the idea of being the only black person there.

★★★

I was glad to be home. I was beginning to feel ill, Priya had worn me out with all that shopping. But, if I was really honest I think it was all that chat about Sukhi's wedding that had done me in. I was convinced that Arun hadn't said one little dickie-bird about it. The way Priya was carrying on, he should have at least mentioned it. It sounded like something out of this world.

My room was like a pigsty but I couldn't be bothered to sort it out. Flopping on the unmade bed, the only thing I had the energy for was to think.

Why hadn't Arun mentioned it? Maybe it wasn't as big a deal as Priya had made out. Or perhaps, if I went, I would have to meet up with Arun's parents – that I did not relish. I think if he had said something about it I probably would have said no. But he hadn't, and I wanted to know why.

We had arranged to meet outside Seven Kings Park, at the Aldborough Road gates, northside. It was only a stone's throw away from my house, across the dual carriageway, just far enough so that none of my family could catch me out. It was proving too much to keep trekking to Aunt Melda's just for Arun to pick me up, so we decided this was much better.

Just as I was leaving, Mum collared me.

'A word in your ear, young lady.' She beckoned me into her bedroom.

'She knows,' was the first thought that jumped into my mind. Had someone told her? I didn't know what to do. Perhaps I should come clean and tell her – but I had to meet Arun in ten minutes. This was not the right time.

'Mum, I'm just going out.'

'This won't take two seconds.'

'But Mum, I know your two seconds – they could mean two hours!'

I walked into her room. The bay window was open and a gentle breeze was blowing the net curtains – well, they weren't really net. They were made of some other stuff that cost the same amount as a return trip to the moon, or so Dad says!

Mum sat on the bed and patted it. I sat next to her. It seemed ages since we had had a good old chat with each other. In the past I would be bouncing around on the bed and Mum would be telling me off. Things had changed. Quietly Mum said, 'Where are you off to, Rell?'

You know something, I really wanted to tell her, but for the life of me, I couldn't. I don't know why.

'Out.'

Mum took a deep breath.

'Yes, I gathered that you were going out, but where?'

My mouth was dry. 'With a friend.'

'Which one? Priya? Helena? Eh . . .'

'A friend from work.'

Pursing her lips, not in anger but in deep thought, Mum was trying to be as diplomatic as possible, I could tell.

'Is there something you want to tell me, Rell?'

We looked at each other, neither trusting ourselves to talk.

'Listen, Mum, I'm fine. I'm not up to any skulduggery, like drug-taking or drinking. I'm not sleeping with any guy, it's just – well, it's just that I'm . . .' I couldn't get the words out. What was wrong with me? I didn't think that Mum would be against Arun because he was Asian, it's just that I wasn't ready to tell her yet.

'Okay, Rell. You're my only daughter and I trust you. I don't think you're involved in anything dangerous, but you be careful now.'

Jumping up, I gave Mum a quick kiss on the cheek. 'See you later, Mum.' I made a dive for the door, zoomed down the stairs and before I knew it I was at the traffic lights waiting to cross the road. I could sense Mum's eyes on me, but I didn't want to turn back. The lights seemed to be taking for ever.

Walking under the subway to the park, I kept going over the conversation I had had with Mum. It seemed ridiculous now that I hadn't told her about Arun. Mum had been really cool and calm when we spoke, but I knew that it wouldn't be very long before she called me in for another 'chat', especially if I carried on being mysterious. Soon she would want some answers, or she would start talking about grounding and all that rubbish and Dad would back her up. You would think I was four years old!

As soon as I saw Arun's car, I walked more quickly. I made up my mind then and there I would tell Mum about Arun.

So that was settled. Now I could get this wedding business sorted out.

'Hi,' I said as I climbed up into a Vitara four by four. Arun kissed me on the lips.

'What, another car?' I laughed.

'I told you, we have about six between the family, so I have to drive whatever is available.' He smiled at me. 'You look beautiful tonight.'

'Thank you.' I was learning to accept his compliments.

'We are off to Daphne's.'

'Who's she?'

'She has a restaurant in west London. I've made a reservation, so we are expected.'

And what a place it turned out to be. I saw a few faces that I had only seen before on TV. The menu didn't even have a price list. From what I could see, people paid with plastic – usually the American Express Gold Card. The atmosphere was reeking with money – I could sense it all around like an invisible thread that wound itself around you, pulling you in.

As I sat facing Arun, I could hardly believe I was there. I had never been one to daydream about living the rich life. When I saw programmes on the telly or read magazine articles about people with loads of dosh, I could never see myself in the picture at all – yet here I was rubbing shoulders with the very same people. Amazing!

After the meal, which to tell the truth wasn't big enough – and wasn't that tasty in my opinion – I thought I would broach the subject of Sukhi's wedding.

'So when is Sukhi getting married?' I came out with it just like that!

'Sukhi, Sukhi?' Arun looked at me, puzzled.

'Yes, your cousin, remember, the one who's getting married to Harjinder.' Priya had made sure that she filled me in on all the details.

Arun tried to mask his surprise.

'Oh, that Sukhi! Quite soon.'

He saw the look on my face and flinched. I sat up straight.

'Well?'

'Well what?'

'When exactly is she getting married?'

'In a few weeks' time.'

'Arun, please refresh my memory – did you tell me about it?'

Quietly he said no.

'Will I be going?' I could have bitten my tongue.

We stared at each other, neither of us saying a word.

He batted the ball into my court. 'Do you want to go?'

I slung it back. 'Do you want me to go with you?'

The people around us continued in their pursuit of conversation, food and drink, while for Arun and me time had stopped.

'Priya again, eh?'

'What do you mean by that?' I had to stick up for my friend even if she'd been trying to stir it.

'As soon as you said that you and Priya were meeting up for lunch to reconcile your relationship I knew that she would try to cause us problems.'

'What has this got to do with Priya? What I want to know is why didn't *you* tell me about it? I felt foolish when she was going on and on about it and I couldn't say anything.'

'So I was right. Listen to me, Rell, I didn't mention it to you because I didn't think you would be interested. Asian weddings are a long process and most people there will be Asian, talking Punjabi, and for most of the time

66

you would probably be on your own, because as part of the family I have to circulate and speak to people.'

'Priya will be there.'

That stopped him.

'So what are you saying – that you want to come?'

'Maybe.' I knew I was being difficult, but what kept popping into my head was the thought that maybe he was ashamed of me.

'Is that a yes or a no?'

'It's a maybe.'

He leaned over to me and whispered, 'Well, let me know, and I'll get you sorted out.'

'What do you mean, sorted out?'

'Well, you'll have to wear a *shalwar-kameez*.'

'A what?'

'A *shalwar-kameez*.'

'What's that?

'A traditional Punjabi suit.'

'Can't I just go in ordinary dress?'

He looked at me.

'Anyway, I only said that I *might* want to go.'

'You'll have to let me know soon. I'll have to have you kitted out right.'

I nodded.

We spent the rest of the evening driving around London, and then we parked up at the Embankment. Holding hands, we strolled along the bridge to the South Bank. The night was cool and balmy. There were other couples doing just as we were. It seemed so unreal, as though we were playing a part in a film or something and THE END would pop up and the credits would roll.

'Arun, I'm going to tell my mum about us,' I said.

'Yeah, well, you said you were thinking about it.'

'Mmm. She spoke to me this evening before I came out. She was fishing around as to what I was up to, and I thought to myself, why don't I tell her the truth? Except I couldn't quite bring myself to do it just then.'

'What do you think her reaction will be?' he asked.

I shrugged my shoulders. 'I don't know. But I don't think she'll go mad or anything. She'll probably want to meet you.'

'Oh no,' he laughed. Turning to me, he pointed his finger and said in a falsetto voice, '"Now you listen to me, young man, make sure you look after my daughter." "Yes, Mrs Bailey." "And no hanky-panky . . ."'

Screaming with laughter, I squealed, 'No hanky-panky! Where did you get those words from?'

Pretending to be offended, he said, 'Isn't that what your mum would say?'

'Course not!'

'Okay then. "Please do not pressure my daughter to have sex with you as I have no desire to be a grand-mother yet. And do not try and seduce her by giving her drugs or alcohol."'

I held on to my stomach. I couldn't stop laughing. Arun laughed along with me, but after a while he said, 'It wasn't that funny, Rell.'

Breathlessly I told him why it was cracking me up. 'My dad, that's just the sort of thing my dad would say!'

Now he burst out laughing. 'Really?'

'Yeah, that's what's so funny, you were spot on.'

By the time we got back to the car it was 12.30.

'Come on, let's get you home.' Arun gunned the engine and the Vitara took off. There was quite a bit of traffic and I noticed that again people stared at us. I didn't know if it was the car or us, being different. Since I had had that conversation with Irene at work, I noticed that it wasn't just black or Asian people that gave us a second look. Even white people turned and stared as though we were an apparition or something. Thinking about it, I wondered if most people were uncomfortable with the idea of mixing up the races. People think you should stick to your side of the fence and that way there won't be any trouble. But that's not the point. I still thought it was important for black people to love each other. That didn't mean, though, that Irene was right to think we should keep everyone trapped in little compartments. It depended, I suppose, on who was being protected from what and why. Anyway, you can come from the same race, the same background, the same family even, but problems will still come up because everyone is unique and differences will always arise. Look at Trenton and me – we're brother and sister, but we still have some heavy disagreements, often borderline fights. Yet we love each other, and if anyone said anything bad about me to him or vice versa, it would be murderation time!

Arun covered my hand with his. 'Tell me, what are you thinking about?'

'About people.'

'What about people?'

'How different we all are. There are no two people that are alike.'

'What about twins?'

'All right, they may look alike, but I bet their parents or people close to them can tell the difference, and their personalities won't be the same. I'm sure even animals are different when they seem to look the same – sheep, for instance. I bet they've got different personalities.'

'Wow, this is a heavy-duty conversation! Here am I thinking romantic thoughts – you're beside me, it's a lovely night – and you want to talk about sheep?'

Grinning, I said, 'I thought that's what attracted you to me, my mind.'

'You're right. Now let's discuss the chemical synapse in brain malfunction, and the release of enzymes causing depression.'

'Yes, let's. I was reading about the very same thing in a medical journal just the other day.'

'Really?' he teased. 'And what did it say?'

'Hmm, it said . . .' I was stalling for time.

'Yessss?'

'It said that women were less prone to brain malfunction because, being much more highly complex creatures, their brains were more sophisticated and superior to those of males. Mind you, it's nothing new. We females have known that all along, but it's only now that men are grudgingly admitting the truth.'

'I'm impressed. Even though it's a lot of nonsense, and totally untrue! It's the other way round, Rell.'

I smiled at him. We've got a really good thing going, I thought. 'The truth always hurts, eh?'

Arun dropped me off at the corner and waited until I was at my door, then he drove past and waved.

***

As I brushed my teeth, I thought back over the evening. I had never felt the way that I did towards Arun with any of my other boyfriends. Sighing, I crept into bed. Florida seemed so far away! I didn't want to go and leave Arun, but I knew that Aunt Melda would freak out if I said I wasn't going.

Anyway, at least this wedding situation hadn't caused any problems between Arun and myself. I wondered about Priya. Had she deliberately tried to stir up trouble? Perhaps I should be more careful when I talked to her about Arun.

Little did I know it was too late.

Seven

'How much yu have inna yur suitcase, Rell?'

'There is absolutely no room, Aunt Melda, I've told you a million times. I'm having to sit on it just to do it up.'

'Me sure yu haven't pack it up properly. Me will have to pass by yur house an check it out.'

It was like talking to a brick wall. Aunt Melda had phoned me early in the morning, when I was still catching up on my beauty sleep, to find out if I had packed for Florida as she still had a thousand things to take that couldn't fit into her already overloaded cases. I didn't want to go over to see her so early, but Mum said I shouldn't come in late if getting up in the morning was going to be such a big deal. So here I was, tussling with Aunt Melda and her 'bigger than life' suitcases. I closed my eyes and yawned, settling back into the armchair as

Aunt Melda tried to achieve the impossible with her packing.

'Hmm . . . If me just push dat back, an roll dat up and . . .'

'I don't want to go.' The thought hit me like a sledge-hammer right between the eyes. I sat bolt upright, looking at Aunt Melda as though she could read my mind and know the thought that I'd had.

Reasoning with myself, I tried to be a bit more positive.

Look, the break will do you good. No Sainsbury's, no Trenton, no Mum and Dad, no boring England – no Arun.

Don't be silly! We've only been dating for such a short while, a few weeks away from each other might do us both good, and we'll be so eager to see each other again . . . As they say, absence makes the heart grow fonder.

'Rell, me is going to have to send a barrel, unless me take a next suitcase and pay de extra when me check in.'

'Aunt Melda, why are you taking so much stuff? All those clothes and shoes – I doubt if you'll wear them all.'

'But it's not fe me to wear, some is to stay there for when we go fe good.'

'Eh? You told me you weren't going to go for a long long time, if at all, so what's the point?'

Straightening herself up, Aunt Melda looked at me and said, 'Chile, yu is too young to understand bout man an wife.' She looked as though she was going to say some more but the phone rang.

'Hello, de Edwards residence, can I help yu?'

Aunt Melda's telephone manner always cracks me up.

I wanted to laugh.

Turning to me she said, 'It's yur mudda.'

Rolling my eyes, I took the receiver from Aunt Melda. 'Yes, Mum?'

'Rell, can you come home now . . .'

'But Mum, I'm helping Aunt Melda . . .'

'I want you here, Rell. Take a cab and I'll pay when you get here . . .'

'Mum . . . Mum . . .' The phone at the other end clicked in my ear.

'Aunt Melda, I've got to go home, something has happened . . .'

'What is it, chile?'

'I don't know, but Mum says I've got to get a cab right away. Have you got a number?'

'Me can drive yu, yu know?'

I knew what Aunt Melda's driving was like and so did Mum – that's why she said that I was to get a cab.

'No, it's okay. Mum said she'll pay for it at the other end. I'd better go.'

The journey seemed to take for ever. I told the driver that I was in a hurry, but he was too busy talking on his mobile phone to hear me. He must've thought I was a tourist because he was cruising along, without a care about me, *and* he took the long way. Mum had been mysterious on the phone, but whatever it was, it sounded like trouble.

The cab driver couldn't pull up outside my house, so he double-parked. He promptly told me how much I owed him, which was the quickest thing he had done since I got into his car, and when I told him the money was inside, he wanted to start some big argument. I didn't bother to get into any situation with him, just jumped out of the car and made a dash for the house. Mum opened the door before I got there.

'How much is it?'

'He wants £4. 50.'

'£4. 50! He's joking, isn't he? Hold on, let me see him.'

'Mum . . .'

But it was too late. She was already near the gate and he was on the other side of it. They started to haggle over the money. I couldn't believe it. Here we were in the middle of some catastrophe, and Mum was making a song and dance out of the cab fare. I walked into the hallway. There was Trenton looking at me in a strange sort of way, and shaking his head.

'Trent, what's going on?'

Instead of answering me, he turned and walked into the kitchen. Puzzled, I followed him.

'What is it, Trent?'

'Come into the front room, young lady,' said Mum behind me.

Dad was sitting by the window. 'Sit down,' he said.

For such a hot day I felt very cold. Something was mega-wrong, and from what I was picking up in the airwaves, I was part of the 'emergency'. My heart was beating so loud it seemed like it wanted to jump through my ribs and bounce out into the room.

'Right,' said Mum, 'let's start at the beginning.'

Trenton came into the room and closed the door. I suddenly felt very sick and very claustrophobic. I wanted to jump through the window. That seemed my only possible route of escape.

Dad said, 'This friend that you have been seeing recently, who is it?'

So they knew about Arun, but why were they holding me in this kangaroo court? I felt pretty sick, but I knew I might as well tell them the truth.

'Arun.'

'It's true then!' shouted Trenton. 'I don't believe it! You've been going out with *him*!'

He sounded so incredulous that I had to say something.

'Yeah, and what's wrong with that?'

Mum jumped in. 'So why was it such a big secret? You'd told us about the meal out after the barbecue, so why all the mystery after that? You've been going out and coming in at all hours . . .'

'I have not been coming in at all hours. I've made sure that it's not been . . .'

'Listen to me when I'm talking to you!' Mum shouted.

'Did he tell you to keep it secret? That nasty young man . . .'

'You can't just blame him, Bertie. I've tried to treat Sorrelle like an adult and let her tell me in her own time what she was up to, but now I find out how she's been carrying on . . .'

'But Mum, I was planning to tell you . . .'

'When? Christmas?'

'No, actually, today.'

Sardonically Mum laughed. 'That is convenient. Today, huh?'

'It's true, I was.'

'Arun Basra, I can't believe it!' Trenton said. Looking first at Mum, then at Dad, he started to tell them about Arun. He said he flashed his money around and got all the girls after him and that he went through them like a large bottle of Syrup of Figs. Then Trenton said that Arun told all his mates about his conquests.

'It's not like that with me,' I said. 'Anyway, I think you're exaggerating.'

Deadly serious, he looked at me and said, 'No, it's true.'

'It's not like that with me and him!'

'Oh yeah?'

'Yeah. Are you going to tell the whole of east London about you and Zara?' That caught him off guard.

'But we're different.'

'And so are we.'

'Let's get back to the issue at hand,' said Dad.

Mum pointed her finger at me, a tirade of hot words pouring from her lips. 'Arun's mum and dad and grand-mother have just been round here . . .'

'What?' I shouted. 'What for?'

'What for? What for? To protect the honour of their precious son! It all happened on the doorstep, so the whole street knows. In fact, the news has probably already hit the West Indies via the Internet, and we have you to thank for bringing shame and disgrace upon this family!'

'It was shameful,' said Trenton, who now seemed to be relishing the whole thing.

'They didn't want to come in, we being black,' Dad said. 'When they found out that Arun has a *black* girl-friend, who has been at *their* house, eating *their* food, sitting in *their* car, with *their* son, they were furious. It was the biggest sin he could have committed.'

Very solemnly Dad spoke again. 'Rell, I don't mind you having a boyfriend.' For Dad to say that, this situation must be cutting him deep. I couldn't even begin to get my brain round it. 'And the fact that he is Asian . . .' Dad stretched out his arms as an indication that it wasn't a problem. 'We lived among many Asian people in Jamaica. But when those people came to our house, begging us to stop our daughter from seeing their wonderful son, because they were fearful that he was going to get contaminated or something . . .'

'No,' I whispered.

'Yes!' Dad shouted. 'Yes, if you were Asian and from another religion, that would be bad. If you were white, that wouldn't be so good, but *black*, that's the worst, the lowest of the low.'

'Bertie,' Mum said softly. 'I'm not sure that's what they meant . . .'

'The thing is, Rell,' Trenton interjected, 'Arun's parents are nice. I've been to their house many times. They were always courteous and polite, they couldn't do enough for me. They were more than surprised when they realised that you were my sister.'

'But the bottom line is this, they do not want you and Arun seeing one another again, ever. Right? That was the only thing that I had to agree with them about. Forget the boy,' said Dad. 'You are worth more than them and their son and their big house in Chigwell and every penny they have in the bank!' And with that, Dad got up and walked out. I could see that the whole episode had stressed him out. It wasn't long before we heard the door slam.

'Trent, haven't you got something to do?'

'Mum, why can't you just say that you want to talk to Rell woman to woman, or mother to daughter, and I'll go?'

'Trent, get out please!'

'But Mum, what have you got to say that hasn't already been said? I want . . .'

'Out!' barked Mum.

When the door closed, Mum sat down in the armchair that Dad had vacated. The heat, plus the hot words spoken, caused the room to be very oppressive. No windows were open and I didn't want to get up to do it, or ask Mum, so I just sat there with rivulets of sweat running down my back. It was awful.

Mum finally looked at me. She seemed sad.

'Have you slept with him?'

'No!' The word tore out of my mouth. I was shocked at Mum asking me that.

'Don't look so shocked. What did you expect? I suspected that you were seeing someone, and I hoped that you would tell me. The fact that you didn't –' She held her hand up so that I couldn't interrupt her. 'I thought that this relationship was perhaps special to you and that you would tell me in your own time. Then I started to worry. Why weren't you telling us? I was planning to confront you, but this – this has knocked me for six.'

'Mum, I was going to tell you today, honest. But what with having to go to Aunt Melda's first thing, there wasn't any time.'

'I gave you the opportunity to tell me yesterday, but

you were in too much of a hurry.'

'That's right, I was. I was meeting Arun, and I didn't want to tell you in two seconds, then dash off. I wanted to tell you when we both had time, and I wanted to sort out my feelings so that when we spoke it would be from my heart.'

Mum sat looking at me for a while. I kept quiet.

'Anyway, his family have made it clear that you both have to stop seeing each other and, to be truthful, I have to agree with them. They are absolutely opposed to your being together and I don't want any more unpleasantness.'

'I can't stop seeing him, Mum . . .'

'Did you hear me? You've only been seeing him for a short while, so you can't tell me that you're going to miss him, or that you have this undying love for him, because that's rubbish.'

'It's not rubbish, we do feel for each other.' I was trying to tell Mum what I felt inside, but it sounded hollow in my ears.

'Rell, this is just puppy love. There's no substance to it, no depth. You probably liked the flash cars, and the money he was spending on you. You'll get over it. It's no big deal. Anyway, you're off to Florida soon and you'll probably meet some Will Smith or Wesley Snipes look-alike and all thoughts of Arun will fly out of your head.'

Quietly I said, 'No they won't, because I'm not going to Florida.'

Mum stood up, brushing aside what I had just said. 'You had better sort out that suitcase of yours. Have you packed it properly? Once it goes through the conveyor belt, those handlers just chuck it any which way. If the case splits, you will really have problems on your hands.'

Now I knew Mum wasn't deaf. She had chosen not to pay me any mind, not to have heard what I said, so, plucking up a bit more courage, I said it again.

'Mum, I thought about it today and especially now, after this fiasco, I'm not going to Florida.'

Mum leaned across to me and with our noses almost touching she said, 'Listen, you are still a child who clearly doesn't know her own mind. And I'm telling you that you are to put that boy out of your stupid head once and for all and you *are* going to Florida, even if I have to drag you by your hair and stick you on the plane myself, so forget that foolishness.'

She left the room.

Hot tears fell out of my eyes and splashed down my face. Even when I closed my eyes, the tears still kept coming.

What a nightmare. What was I going to do?

An arm encircled me. I looked up and saw Trenton.

'Oh Trent, what a mess. What am I going to do?'

'Rell, if I was you I would give Arun a miss. He's a nice guy, one of the better ones, and I'm sure he's treated you great, but the thing is, after what happened today, there's no point in trying to go on with it. Mum and Dad were so livid, I thought Dad was going to knock Mr Basra out. I had to jump in between them. And the way the grand-mother was carrying on, you would have thought someone had died. It was terrible. Florrie from across the road actually came out of her front door with her arms crossed and stared at us. It was shameful.'

I groaned and cried at the same time.

'Do you want me to give him a message?' Trent asked.

'No, I want to speak to him myself.'

'Rell, listen to me. If I were you I would forget the whole thing, and besides, by the time Arun's family have put the pressure on him, I don't think he's going to want to see you either.'

'No, I don't believe that!'

'Rell, c'mon, face facts.'

Sniffing now, the fog in my head slowly clearing away, I knew that I had to see Arun to talk things through. We'd only been dating each other a short time, but I knew what we had was special. It sounded dry even as I thought it, but it was true.

I needed time to think. I left Trent in the kitchen and went up to my room. I sat on the floor amidst piles of discarded clothes and wondered what to do. Then it suddenly came to me that I didn't know how Arun's parents had found out about us. Did he tell them, or did someone else?

The only person that knew about us in any depth, and knew Arun's parents, was Priya.

No, I thought, she couldn't have, she wouldn't.

Did she phone them up or send them an anonymous letter? I couldn't believe it. But was it really her? Maybe someone who knew Arun and his family had seen us out together, then gone right back and told his parents. That seemed more logical to me.

My first plan of action, then, was to speak to Arun and to discuss what was going to happen now.

I hoped and prayed that Priya wasn't the informer.

I really hoped she wasn't.

Eight

'It's so humid. I feel like a sweat bubble, trapped under someone's armpit.'

'Don't be so disgusting, Rell. Why can't you just say that you feel hot?' Mum said.

It was almost one o'clock and we had just finished our breakfast! The events of yesterday were still very fresh in my mind. I couldn't or more truthfully didn't want to discuss them with Mum. I was functioning on autopilot, saying and doing things as naturally as possible. It was strange, but somehow I was managing to talk about most things while my mind was elsewhere.

Arun.

I could see his face, hear his voice, smell him even. Yet I had to keep him locked in my heart, the door firmly closed.

He hadn't phoned me yet. I wasn't sure if that was a

good sign or a bad one. I wanted to phone him, but I would have to whisper and pretend that I was talking to someone else. I knew that my family would be suspicious about who I was talking to and if they knew it was Arun, well, it would be pure aggravation. It wasn't worth it.

But it was freaking me out, not knowing what was happening to him. Was he all right? Was he angry? Had his parents drugged him and had him shipped off abroad? The suspense was killing me.

'Why don't you sit in the garden for a bit, Rell?'

'Maybe I will.' I didn't want to commit myself to doing anything. All I wanted was to see Arun.

'I've got to go to work soon. How anyone is expected to work in the heat I don't know.'

'I think I will sit outside for a while.'

Mum smiled at me. 'That's a good idea, the fresh air will do you some good.'

'Fresh air in Newbury Park – are you joking, Mum?'

She laughed.

Actually, lying on the sun lounger soaking up the sun was making me feel a whole lot better, and I was able to think a lot more clearly. I wasn't sure what time Mum would be back home – as a social worker she worked some funny hours, and on top of that she was on call.

I was planning on phoning Arun on his mobile, but not from home. I would go into Ilford and call him from a phone box. I didn't even want to risk phoning him from a payphone nearby in case Trenton saw me. I wasn't sure if he would tell Mum or Dad or not, but I didn't want to risk falling out with any of them so I would have to box clever, and use my head.

I closed my eyes. I wanted to really relax and get my thoughts together, but there was a nasty buzzing fly hovering around me, like I was its potential lunch. It must have been the cocoa butter cream I was wearing. The stupid thing wouldn't leave me alone. There really is no peace for the wicked! I forced myself to think things through. Of course I desperately needed to speak to Arun, but then what? Apart from what he felt, what did I want to do? What we had together felt special, but it was still early days for us. We hadn't had a chance to find out if we really had a future together. It wasn't fair!

I was just thinking of rousing myself into action when who should plonk themselves down beside me but Zara.

'Hi, Rell, how you doing?'

Blinking away my disorientation, I sort of mumbled, 'Hi.' This was the last person I wanted to see. I wanted as much time as I could get to hopefully not only speak to Arun but also to see him.

'The weather's great, isn't it? I love the summer!'

'Eh yeah, it's great.'

'I don't have to spend any money at the shop.'

The girl had lost me already.

'The shop? What are you talking about?' It amazed me that Trenton, who has really got it up there (being big on brain power), had hooked himself up with a dumbo like Zara. It's got to be physical. I mean, they can't have a normal conversation, surely!

'The shop where I use the sun bed. In the summer the sun's natural rays do the job, and I go a nice golden colour and it doesn't cost me a thing.'

She's mad.

'I'm glad I came into the world as I am. All this tanning business, which can definitely damage your health, would be too much for me.'

'You're lucky. I wish I was permanently this colour.' She pointed to her arm. 'It's such a rich colour and it goes with most other colours. When I'm a pasty white, I look so boring. I *feel* boring.'

'Hmm.' I wanted to go – now.

'Well Zara, I'll have to love you and leave you.'

'Oh, where are you off to?'

'Ilford.'

'Really? I need some stuff in Alders. I tell you what, I'll come with you.' She went into the house shouting for Trenton. I tried to jump up quickly to tell her that I wanted to go alone, but it sort of all happened in a flash and the next thing I knew Trenton was saying what a good idea it was for us two to go shopping together.

The fumes that were coming out of the exhaust pipe of the bus were nothing to the fumes that were building up inside me. This was a put-up job if ever I had seen one. All that talk about 'tanning' and the 'nice weather' chat was just to find out what I was doing so they could mess up my plans.

Trenton must have been instructed by my parents to keep tabs on me, and Zara was in on it.

She was totally oblivious to my mood. She chatted away a hundred to the dozen, and what she was talking about only the window, and the back of the head of the person that was sitting in front of us, know. I was racking my brains to think how I could get rid of her so that I could at least phone Arun.

We got off the bus outside Barclays Bank and began to walk towards the Exchange.

Two hours later, I felt close to tears. Zara was sick. She was a shopaholic. It was a disease. We must have been into every shop, barring Kwik Save and Sainsbury's, in Ilford. I'm not the sort of person to swear, but I could sense that horrible feeling building up inside of me, and I wanted to spew it out all over Zara. My feet had swollen up, there seemed to be grime all over my body and I just wanted to get away from Zara, Ilford, my family, everything.

'Do you fancy a salad from Pizza Hut, Rell?' Zara grabbed my arm and tried to drag me towards the restaurant.

That did it.

'No, no, no! I've had it up to here with you and your nonstop mouth! I followed you all over Ilford, so why don't you just . . .'

Her voice changed, and became really serious. 'Look Rell, please come into Pizza Hut. I want to talk to you, I want to help you.'

'Help me, help me do what?' I had started to say and tears were rolling down my face. I felt dreadful. I let her lead me into Pizza Hut. Waves of helplessness washed over me.

We sat down at a booth. I wanted to stop crying, but I couldn't.

'It's not fair. No one understands,' was all I could say.

Zara, for the first time all day, didn't seem to have anything to say either. She just patted my hand. After a while she gave me a Wet Wipe to clean my face, followed by a tissue.

By the time our drinks came I had stopped crying, but depression and hopelessness were hanging around me, waiting to pounce.

'Feeling a bit better?'

I shrugged. How could I feel better? I had no answers to the questions that were running around inside me like an unbroken circuit.

'You need to speak to Arun.'

I nodded, my head hanging down.

Zara began to fumble in her bag, then said, 'Here, use this.'

She had her mobile phone in her hand!

'I, eh . . .' I wasn't sure if this was a trick and she was going to report back to Trenton.

'Don't worry, this is between you and me.'

I took the phone and quickly dialled his number. It rang once.

'Hi, it's me.' I said. And that was about all the chance I got to say anything, He started to talk and didn't stop.

'He wants to see me!' I hissed to Zara.

'Tell him, if he's quick, he can meet us here, at the Hut,' she hissed back. This girl was a surprise a minute.

I made the arrangement with Arun and then gave her back her phone.

'Why are you doing this?' I asked. I still felt a bit suspicious.

'Because I've been there. Even though my parents aren't together and don't agree on anything, there is one thing they see eye to eye on. Me.' She pointed to herself. 'Dating a black guy is way out of line. But the funny thing is, my mum's boyfriend can't see what the problem is. He reckons that as long as I'm not taking drugs, or in danger in any way, my parents should just lay off!'

'But you've been going out with Trent for some time now. I never knew there was a problem with your parents. How do they feel about it now?'

'My dad doesn't want me to bring Trent to his house, but that suits me. because he's a very ignorant man. His new girlfriend is only a few years older than me and she's thick. My mum, now that she can see that I'm all right, is slowly coming round. She said to me the other day that she thought Trent was quite good-looking. Coming from her, that's one big compliment.'

I couldn't eat the garlic bread when it came, but Zara had no such problem. The plate was clean in what seemed like two seconds.

Zara has been going out with my brother for five months and even though I thought I knew her, I never really *knew* her.

I sat there waiting for Arun. All my nerves were tingling and I was finding it hard to sit still. Zara must have some powerful invisible antennae because she said to me, 'Relax. Don't let him find you a bag of nerves. He must be taking this hard as well. I mean, this isn't an easy situation, is it?'

She was right on that score.

My mouth felt as though I had swallowed a handful of sand. I took a sip of my drink. A thought just occurred to me. I had to ask Zara something.

'Zara, you're not going to tell Trent about this, are you?'

She noted the fear in my voice. 'Don't be silly, of

course I won't tell him. Look Rell, just trust me. Don't be frightened, face it head on. It can't get any worse than this.'

I couldn't answer her. I knew things could in fact get a lot worse.

Aeons of time seemed to go by. My eyes were glued to the door. At last it burst open. Arun came dashing in, breathless, his eyes scanning the place, until they landed on me. My heart jumped as he made his way to me.

He slid in beside me and just looked at me. Neither of us spoke.

'Excuse me, but do you think it's wise to be sitting here, hmm, so public?'

Arun jumped back as though he had just been electrocuted. 'You're right. Let's go.'

Zara, mouth full of food, mumbled, 'Just give me a minute, and I'll be with you. We've got to get the bill.'

'Don't worry, I'll pay. You both make your way out of here. Turn right, the Vitara's just there.'

Shoving another spoonful of pasta into her mouth, Zara stood up and collected her bags. I was at the door by the time she had wiped her mouth and taken a couple of gulps of her drink, and I was standing by the Vitara by the time Arun came out. We all jumped in, with me at the back and Zara at the front. No one said a word. Arun seemed to know where he was going; the Vitara, effortlessly zoomed along.

Brentwood.

By the time Arun stopped, I didn't care where we were, I just wanted to get out and walk about.

We were outside some shops. Zara seemed to be the

only one who knew what to do. She said, 'I'll do some window-shopping, you both have a chat. I'll give you half an hour, right?' She smiled at us. 'See you later.'

Arun told me to get back in, and drove for a bit until we came to a quiet road, then pulled over.

'Rell,' he said quietly. Then he threw his arms around me. I cried. He held me tighter, saying he was sorry over and over again.

'I don't know what to say, Rell. My parents didn't say anything to me before they visited your home, then, when they came back, they really laid into me. If they had told me what they were going to do, I would have tried to stop them, I promise. At the very least, I would have warned you in advance.'

Sniffing, I said, 'From all accounts it was horrendous. Your family standing yelling on our doorstep.'

He groaned. 'This is why I wanted to pick the right time to tell them. Whoever told them managed to stir things up all right. I can't work out who . . .'

'You can't work out who. The first name to spring to my mind was Priya.'

'Priya? But . . .'

'You know she had her eye on you herself – she made that pretty obvious. You're just the type her parents would go for, and I know she fancies you. I've had this uneasy feeling about her . . .'

Quietly Arun said, 'But she's your friend. Tell me honestly, Rell, do you think that Priya would do this?'

'Yes . . . No . . . I don't know. Oh, Arun, what are we going to do?'

He leaned back in his seat and took a deep breath.

'Carry on doing what we're doing. Keeping a low profile.'

'Keep a low profile? What if someone somewhere sees us and tells either of our parents? Then there will be hell to pay. We've got to do something, but what, I don't know.'

We sat in silence for a while, as our brains searched and searched for a solution. There was none.

'Do you trust Zara?' Arun asked.

'Yeah.' I told him how my day had been. 'I can't get over it. She's the last person I thought would come to my rescue.'

'Thank God for Zara. I was contemplating coming round to your house and sitting in my car until you came out or until I saw all your family leave. Then I was going to ring your bell.'

He leaned forward and kissed me and for that short time all our problems seemed to recede.

'Listen, Rell,' Arun said, 'we have to work out how we can contact each other and how to meet up.'

'I can call you on your mobile. We'll just have to be creative and think of different places and ways to meet.'

He nodded.

Zara and I clambered out of the Vitara in the Apples Gym car park. 'I'll call you tomorrow,' I said to Arun.

Arun drove away and we walked slowly down the road towards my house.

'Zara, I don't know how to thank you, you know.'

'Just don't let on that it was me that got you two together.'

Running my finger across my mouth, I said, 'You better believe it.'

Trenton was in the kitchen stuffing his face when we got in. Zara sat down at the table with him, while I just got a Coke from the fridge and went up to my room.

I opened the window and the cool early evening air slowly breezed in. I sat exhausted on the edge of my bed with my head in my hands and wondered how I had got myself in this mess.

If only.

If only Arun was black.

If only I hadn't agreed to do the barbecue.

If only I hadn't gone on that dinner date with him.

If only I had kept my mouth shut and not told Priya anything.

If only his parents hadn't come round.

I began to pace the room. I remembered how I had always said that mixed relationships were too much bother. I doubted very much if Arun was black that all this nonsense would be going on. We would be happily dating, our parents wouldn't mind too much as long as we weren't mixed up with drugs or drink. No one would be staring at us on the street. Basically, everything would be cool.

And now look at all this mess. I had thrown caution to the wind and gone against my principles and I was plunged in the middle of a mini-war.

For the first time I wondered if I really wanted to go through all this hassle. But then I realised that it wasn't just dating Arun that was causing me problems. I was being told to obey my parents and his, and that wanting to do my own thing, make my own decisions, whatever the consequences, was really not on. But surely that was what growing up, maturing, was really all about? Then again my parents weren't going to see things like that. Arun's parents had rejected me big time, and that was enough for them. As far as they were concerned it wasn't just me who was under attack, it was them as well, and they had principles too!

What was the answer to all this?

By now my head was pounding. Every thought that came into my head led to a shut door, and there was no key to open it.

I didn't want to lie and deceive my parents, but for the moment that was what I was faced with. Maybe Mum was right and this would all fizzle out after a while, but there was something inside me that wasn't going to give up. I had to see this through.

What if we ended up as an item together for ever?

Children?

Mortgage?

Cut off from both parents?

Could we do it? Would we eventually despise each other?

My mind felt like Aunt Melda's bulging suitcase. I wished I could take my head off my shoulders and have a break from all the thinking I was doing.

Thinking about Aunt Melda reminded me about the trip to Florida. I couldn't possibly face it. Unresolved conflict didn't make for a stress-free, peaceful holiday. I wondered if Aunt Melda would understand if I told her I wasn't going. That thought didn't bring a smile to my lips. Going out with Arun was like flinging a pebble into a lake.

The ripples went on and on, getting bigger all the time. I wanted the whole thing sorted out. And now, so that whatever the outcome I would just have to live with it.

Life was a complex business.

I heard Trent shouting, 'Rell! The phone!'

I knew instinctively it was Priya. I didn't want to talk to her, but how could I get out of it? I waited for a bit, trying to think of a way of avoiding her.

'Rell!' Trent was standing at the top of the stairs.

'Yes?'

'Why aren't you answering the phone? Are you okay?'

'Fine. I was just, eh, looking for my slipper. Who is it anyway?'

'It was your buddy, Priya. But she's gone now.'

Relieved, I said quickly, 'Oh really, that's a shame.'

'She said that she was in a rush, she had to do something, but that she's coming round.'

I just looked at him. 'Oh, right.'

'You sure you're okay, Rell?'

I felt so annoyed I couldn't help but snap at Trent. 'Yeah, I'm feeling fantastic, all right?'

Nine

'Yu is de only person dat me can remember dis long time, dat did tell me someting an me can't find a word fi sey.' Aunt Melda's mouth and eyes seemed to grow larger by the second.

I couldn't look at her for long, because of what I thought was misplaced guilt. I had tried to broach the subject of not going to Florida with Mum, but she just wouldn't listen. Dad calls it her 'growing roots and not budging' mood, but it's just plain old stubbornness. So, I thought the next best thing would be to tell Aunt Melda to her face. I really didn't want to, I was sort of hoping that Mum would do it for me, but as she chose not to speak to me about it, that option was proving difficult.

Clearly puzzled, Aunt Melda said again for the tenth time, 'So tell me again as to why yu not going?'

I explained briefly about Arun again. I could see that Aunt Melda was growing more mystified with each word I spoke.

'So this Indian bwoy is yur bwoyfriend, whom yu gwine fi marry?'

'Marry, who mentioned marriage? We are just dating, Aunt Melda.'

'Hmmm, dats what me tink yu sey, an dat's what me can't understand. If him is only yur bwoyfriend dat yu know only dis lickle time, why, tell me, why yu have fi give up dis lovely holiday fi him?'

Sometimes talking to Aunt Melda was like digging a road with a toothpick. How she managed as a teacher, I do not know. She wanted me to explain to her over and over again about the situation with Arun. The bit about his parents coming to my house had her in peals of laughter, but everything else was a mystery. After talking at cross-purposes for a very long time, Aunt Melda laid down the gauntlet.

'Me tell yu something, chile. Me will cancel de vacation fi two weeks. After dat, if yu still don't want to go, me will go alone. Yur mother will have to refund me money.'

That brought me up a bit sharp. 'Refund the fare, you mean?'

Calmly Aunt Melda turned to me and said, 'Oh yes, if yu think dat me is going to dash way my hard-earned money, yu make a sad mistake. If yu want fi mess up yur life fi some young man, dat's fine by me, but not with my money yu don't.'

This was not good news. I couldn't see Mum footing

the bill. I'd have to pay it, but where was I going to get all that money from?

While I was at Aunt Melda's Dad phoned me. I know he was just checking up to make sure I was there, but I never let on to him that I knew what he was doing. Mum, Dad and Trenton were all keeping an eye on me now. I knew they were monitoring my phone calls, and they wanted to know where I was going, who I was with, what time I would home – it was getting on my nerves. Anyway, I was too smart for them, because I was still able to meet up with Arun. Zara was being a tower of strength, covering for me, and helping me meet up with him. If Trenton had ever found out I think he would have sent her packing – more's the pity.

It was now just over a week since the fiasco had started and each day seemed like a year. I was glad it was holiday time. The way I was feeling I certainly wouldn't be able to face school. Mostly I just lazed about the house, anticipating my hours with Arun. The secrecy of our time together seemed to spark up the excitement of it all. Arun was becoming like a highly addictive drug that I couldn't seem to get enough of. The fact that it wasn't a physical relationship made it even more electrifying. We couldn't meet at his cousin's flat any more because Arun suspected his parents were having the place watched. It seemed incredible. The only people I knew who hired private eyes were on TV!

I had purposely not been seeing too much of Priya. That day she came round to my house I didn't want to be near her, let alone tell her what was going on in my life, so I tried to divert her. I suggested we walk to the farm near my house. All the way there she talked and talked. Anger was mounting inside of me, I wanted to thump her. As she chatted, it kept going round and round in my mind that she had caused all these problems I could well do without, and here she was carrying on like butter wouldn't melt in her mouth. This was one of life's lessons for me. Mum had always told me to choose my friends carefully. Mum has one close friend, a woman called Sister Pauline who Mum has known since school. She lives in Clapham and she's a regular church-goer. They don't see each other often but they talk for hours on the phone.

'You see, Rell, when you have people who are close to you, and you see them regularly and they are involved in your life, it's easy to have problems with them somewhere along the line. It's much safer to have a friend who doesn't live too close. Then she can be objective about your problems and there's no fear of her getting too involved.'

When Mum talks like that I know she's speaking from experience, but most of the time I let her advice pass over my head. Now though, as Priya prattled on, I knew what Mum meant.

As we walked across the dry, cracked farmland, I thought of smashing Priya's head until it resembled the ground. She was talking about the wedding and the clothes she had already bought, and how she was finding it difficult to make up her mind what to wear.

'Why don't you wear them all?'

'What?' she said.

'You heard.' I walked off ahead as she slowed down.

99

My anger was smouldering. I was hoping she would say just one wrong word so that I would have an excuse to jump down her throat.

My luck was in.

Just when I was thinking I would never get the truth from her about how Arun's parents knew about me, she confessed all!

'. . . My mum said that my dad was really shocked that Arun was dating you.' She paused to see my reaction, but I wanted to see what else she had to say – and say it she did.

'. . . Anyway, Mum said it was all the fashion now for the colours to mix themselves up. Dad said it wasn't right, and everyone should stick to their own.'

Where had I heard that before?

Then she talked quite openly about how her dad spoke to Arun's father, at the do in the West End hotel, the one held by Sukhi's parents, like my business is any of his business, and how Arun's father went quiet as though he was hearing it for the first time that his son had a black girlfriend. Well, of course, it *was* the first time he was hearing it. He must have been furious!

By the time Priya had finished telling me all about it I had had enough. In the middle of the field under God's sky my only witnesses were a few birds and flies. I was so mad, upset and angry I found it a bit hard to speak at first, and then it just all came out in a rush.

'You, Priya!' I pointed my finger in her face. She looked shocked. 'You took it upon yourself to tell your nosy parents my business and then your foolish dad pushes himself up on Arun's dad like they're in the same league and tells him about me and Arun ...' My lungs felt tight and I was finding it hard to breathe.

'Don't call my dad foolish, Rell. He's a smart man, you know, and Arun's ...'

'Shut up!' I shouted.

Fear began to creep into her eyes.

'You and your family have caused untold problems to me and my family, because of your creepy, big-mouthed dad! Arun's family came round to my house and now everyone's trying to split us up! I've been through hell in the last few days!'

Trying to come across as a bit tough, Priya said, 'Look Rell, I think we had better forget this and talk about something else.'

'Yeah, you're right. This!' And I whacked her with all my might.

To my great surprise, she hit me back.

'Why couldn't you keep your big mouth shut!' I yelled at her. 'You skinny nastiness!'

I kicked hard at the grass around us. She stood staring at me with round eyes. All of a sudden, my anger flowed out of me and was replaced by disgust, sadness and every negative feeling that had nowhere else to go. I stopped kicking and started crying.

Priya was crying too. I sat down in the grass and wept. Never have I felt like this in all my life. To want to attack someone and actually do it was so out of character for me it was frightening. The stress of the last week or so had ended up in this. At this moment in time I could understand how people just lost it and ended up committing murder.

I heard Priya whisper something but I couldn't quite make out what it was. To be truthful I didn't want to hear what she had to say. It couldn't change anything.

'Did you hear me, Rell? I'm sorry. I didn't know how much you would be hurt. I never told my dad, my mum did, and it was only when they came back from the do and I was asking them how it went that Dad just mentioned that he'd had a good talk with Arun's dad and that he was going to put some business his way. He said that he'd sort of mentioned you and Arun and that Arun's dad looked a bit dumbstruck. I didn't think that much of it.' She was wiping her face and sniffing. 'Rell, we shouldn't let this come between us. We are still going to be friends, aren't we?'

I didn't answer her.

If anyone had told me a couple of weeks ago that I was going to attack my best friend I would have laughed. But here I was having just done that.

We walked back to my house in semi-silence. Priya was trying hard to make conversation with me, but I wasn't responding too much.

As we approached my house I turned to her and said, 'I'm sorry, Priya, for going crazy on you.'

'That's all right, Rell, I understand.'

'I think we should call it a night. I'm going to go and have a shower and then go to bed, so there's no point in you coming in tonight. I'll see you later.' I walked up to my front door, turned the key in the lock and let myself in. I didn't stop to see if Priya was still standing there. That was it as far as I was concerned.

But not as far as Priya was concerned. She continued to phone me morning, noon and evening, chatting away nineteen to the dozen. But I felt too hurt to forgive her. She may not have intended to cause trouble for me, but I was in trouble. I'd never had so much hassle in all my life. The more Priya tried to hang on to our friendship the more I wanted to distance myself from her. She was like a toothache, a griping pain that would drive you mad, until you had the tooth extracted.

I told my family that whenever she phoned they should tell her I wasn't in. That was fine by them because my parents thought it was Priya who had helped fix me and Arun up. Trenton knew otherwise, but he was never too hot on her anyway, so the fact that I didn't want much to do with her was okay by him.

The evening after Aunt Melda's I was up in my room, freshly scrubbed on the outside, yet on the inside I still felt unclean thinking about Priya. How could I have ended up fighting? It seemed so odd. But I felt a little bit of satisfaction too. That was what a good old punch-up did, it made you feel better. But it hadn't resolved anything. I still didn't want to be friends with Priya.

Wearily, I got into bed. Arun had given me some photos of him and just looking at them lifted my spirits. Since I had been seeing him, he had grown more and more handsome. We hadn't said that we loved each other, but I could feel it in the air around us when we were together.

How was this all going to end?

I pushed thoughts like that out of my head. They weren't productive, so why spend time and energy on them?

The night before when I had seen Arun he had told me stories which made me feel scared.

We had found this country pub and were having a meal. At first he was making me laugh about things that he had got up to when he was a boy, but then somehow he started to tell me about how things were at home with him.

'You know, Rell, my dad still has people following me. I'm having to get really clever to keep ahead of them.'

I looked around nervously. 'Do you know who they are?'

'Men who work for my dad. He pays them for trailing me, of course, and they'd do anything to keep in my dad's good books. But I know how to give them the slip.'

'I'm glad you do. I have to use my loaf when I want to see you. My dad is still acting a bit strange, but Mum seems to have cooled down. I think that Aunt Melda putting the holiday off for a couple of weeks has helped. Mum says she'll pay the extra money for the reissue of new tickets, but she wants me to pay her back.'

'Don't worry, I'll sort you out, Rell.'

'No, it's okay.'

'No, I want to. After all, in a way it's my fault.'

We held hands across the table. 'My dad says that from now on he only wants me to drive the Mondeo. That's the car that my mum usually drives. It's all part of them slowly twisting my arm to conform to their ways. He hasn't enforced it yet, so I'm still chopping and changing vehicles.'

'At least you have a car to drive, so don't worry about which one. Besides, flash cars are only to attract the opposite sex!' I teased.

'That's not true,' he laughed.

Then he started to tell me about people he knew that had dated the 'wrong' type of person as far as their family were concerned and what had happened to them.

'. . .They are mainly girls, but I have known of a few guys who have disappeared – supposedly gone back to India or Pakistan. They get married off to people they only meet on the wedding day. One guy I knew was dating a girl of a lower caste. His parents couldn't cope with the shame of it. They didn't mess about. They spiked his tea one day and got him down to the airport and the next thing he knew, when he was back in his right mind, he was on a plane bound for Delhi.'

Fear began to spring up like a green shoot in spring. 'You don't think your parents will do that to you, do you?'

'No, I don't think so. I think if they thought you and me were really serious, leading up to marriage or something, they might start plotting, but we should be okay for the moment.'

We were going to have dessert when two white couples sat at the table next to us. They started talking in loud voices, making sure that we could hear them.

'I don't know what this country is coming to,' said one of the guys. He didn't look much older than Arun.

Then one of the girls piped up. 'When the blacks and the Pakis start getting together, this country will be heading for big trouble.'

They were obviously talking about us. I wanted to retaliate and start telling them about themselves.

'Come on, Rell, let's go,' said Arun.

That annoyed me. I didn't know what was happening to me lately, but I was becoming quite aggressive.

As we roared off in the Vitara, one of the girls stuck two fingers up. I was itching to do the same back, but I felt that Arun wouldn't have been impressed by that.

'What is wrong with these people? They're mad!'

Philosophically Arun answered, 'What you have to understand is that when people see other nationalities coming into their country and doing much better than they ever could, seeing as they themselves don't have the capability or the drive, then jealousy consumes them. They start thinking that if they got rid of the other races they would be able to do better and have what was left behind. Of course it doesn't work like that. If we weren't here working so hard for every penny we've got, those people still wouldn't be able to get what we have.'

'But they don't see it like that.'

'You mean they don't want to see it like that.'

There was a photo of Arun that was my favourite. He was leaning against a tree, casually dressed, shirt over his jeans, with one hand in his pocket. He was smiling into the camera. That photo really captured what I saw when I looked at Arun. Putting aside the money and stuff, he was just a nice-looking guy.

I looked at my watch. It was only 9.30. We had planned to meet up tomorrow afternoon and go for a picnic. I was supposed to be working as it was a Wednesday, but now that I had cancelled my holiday to Florida, I just took the day as annual leave. I would leave home in my uniform, but change in some loos along the way. My mum was working late and so I knew she wouldn't be going into Sainsbury's, and Dad and Trenton thought that shopping was women's work. For once I agreed with them, as it would keep them out of the store.

Snuggling down under the sheet, I thought about the way my relationship with Arun was going. I was happy with it, as long as I kept thoughts of getting caught out of my mind. Now that I had eliminated Priya from my business, and we were being careful about how and where we met, I felt that our relationship might go somewhere. The trouble is, when you think you've got a thing sussed something always happens to blow away all your carefully laid plans. You try to keep thinking positively as all the good books say you should. Thinking positively will make things positive, that's what they say, but that's a lot of rubbish. Who can see round corners? Who can really know what's going to happen from one minute until another?

No one.

What a picnic it turned out to be.

Ten

'Rell, I won't be back until about nine tonight. I think your dad will be back earlier than me. Now, will you be all right?' The look Mum gave me really said, 'I hope we can trust you not to go off with Arun.'

'No problem, Mum.' I smiled confidently at her.

'Make sure you're not late for work today. What are you going to do afterwards – meet up with Priya?'

'Eh, maybe.'

'Okay then, I'll see you later.'

I hadn't really let on to anyone that me and Priya were not friends any more. Even Priya didn't seem to know because she still phoned me. What for I do not know. I had started taking her calls again, civilly enough, but our relationship just wasn't the same.

Mum was off to some conference in Birmingham for the day and Dad and Trenton were conveniently out too, so I had the whole house to myself.

I knew that Mum suspected that I was still seeing Arun, but she didn't have any proof. I heard her and Dad talking about me in their bedroom. I didn't really like to be eavesdropping on their conversation, but considering it was about me, I thought it best I have a listen.

'. . . She is, you know, Bertie.'

'Are you sure?'

'If you mean do I have any proof, no. But I feel in my heart that she is still meeting up with him.'

'Well, let's have it out with her. If you think that after all she has put us through I am going to allow her to come and go freely, while she is still seeing that boy, you make a sad mistake. Listen, Donna, I haven't raised any child of mine to have no self-respect. This world is a hard place, and twice as hard if you're black. When anybody, no matter what colour, race, religion, I don't care, whatever, tries to bring you down and rejects you just because you're black, then as far as I'm concerned, you say goodbye to that person.'

'But to be fair, honey, it isn't Arun that is rejecting Rell, it's his family. From what Trenton has told me Arun didn't even know that they had come round here until they got home and told him.'

'It doesn't matter. He is their son. If you think that anything decent is going to come of their relationship, forget it. He's just using my baby daughter, and that hurts, Donna, that cuts me deep. I don't want her associating with him, in any shape or form.'

'At least I know she's not sleeping with him, which gives me some peace of mind. But I do agree with you,

Bertie, and I'm letting you know now, if ever I get some concrete evidence that Rell is seeing him I'll be really hot and mad, and who knows what I'll do to her.'

I didn't hang around to hear any more. That was enough.

Relaxing in a lukewarm bath was a great way to think. And was I thinking. I had told Arun that I would meet him in Romford. It was less likely that we would be seen by anyone we knew there. I was glad that I had overheard my parents talking. At least I knew where I stood. I also knew that they knew that I was seeing Arun. I wondered if that was because I was still going out and about. I had tried to come home early but a few times I was a bit late, and yet they hadn't said much to me. They were biding their time. I didn't intend to get caught, though.

I was hoping that both sets of parents would eventually come round, but wasn't holding my breath.

Looking at my body in the bathroom mirror as I covered it with cocoa butter, I wondered what Arun would think if he saw it. I had lost a bit of weight and looked borderline skinny. My stomach was taut like I had been doing press-ups, and the muscles on my legs and arms really stood out. Turning round, I looked at my bottom. It was round and hard like an apple. 'Would you desire me, Arun?' I pouted in the mirror. Suddenly I felt exposed, as though he really could see me. Even though it was a hot day, I felt cold. I quickly darted to my room and got dressed.

Romford was busy. We had decided to meet up outside Debenhams as the car park wasn't too far away. Arun told me that he would provide all the food for the picnic.

Standing by the double doors of Debenhams, I tried to look inconspicuous. I wasn't sure if I was succeeding as most people were on the move, and I was like a statue.

'Hi, Rell.' Arun nearly made me jump out of my skin. He kissed me on the lips. Nervously I looked around. 'Not here! There's so many eyes, you don't know who could be looking at us.'

'Don't worry, we're safe here. Listen, we need some drinks. Let's go into Debenhams and buy a few cans of something.'

Linking arms, we went in. Once we bought the drinks I wanted to get out, but Arun wanted to look around the store.

'No, let's go,' I said. I just didn't feel comfortable. It was like being on public display.

He said he didn't care.

'Come on, we'll be all right here.'

So we trooped off to the women's section and some-how we ended up looking at the bridal wear. Nothing grabbed me, but the thought that Arun was interested made me fantasise that perhaps he did have marriage on his mind. It *was* pure fantasy, but it was only for a few minutes, so it wasn't doing me any harm. A shop assistant with frizzy brown hair and thick, thick mascara that made her eyelashes look like two brushes appeared out of nowhere and asked us when the happy day was going to be. Arun winked at me and said to her, 'We're having a winter wedding, have you got any thermal dresses?'

I burst out laughing.

Before the assistant could answer, an Asian woman I

had seen earlier came up to us.

'Arun Basra,' she said, 'how are you?'

I looked from the woman to Arun to the shop assistant. The very thing I dreaded was now happening. We had been recognised.

Arun said hello and was very polite to her, but she was craning her neck to have a good look at me.

'I've got to go now. Bye!' Arun looked at me and we quickly walked away.

Neither of us spoke. I felt sick. As we walked out of the store the nightmare increased. 'Hi Rell, Arun. What a lovely couple you both make. Where are you off to now?'

Priya.

A ten-ton stone slowly sunk to the pit of my stomach. I didn't want to talk to Priya. What could I say?

Arun said, 'We're just doing some shopping. We'll see you later, Priya.' He took my hand and we legged it.

When we got to the car park I was surprised to see Arun stop at a dark green Mondeo.

'You're driving this now?'

'Yeah, just for a while.'

I could see that he didn't want to talk about it, so I dropped it. We drove to South Weald. I was upset. I had already told Arun that if he had listened to me in the first place about going into Debenhams, none of this would have happened. At first he didn't answer me, but I was more than annoyed and I kept going on.

'All right,' he suddenly shouted. 'You were right and I was wrong, okay?'

'There's no need to shout!' I shouted back at him.

Now where did this mess leave us?

Under the shade of a tree, the air between us had cooled down. A good thing, I suppose, since the day was so hot. I really didn't want the rest of our time together affected by what had happened earlier, but it was difficult to know how to move on.

'So, this woman, does she know your parents well?'

'She's a distant cousin of my mum's.'

'Does she have contact with your mum a lot?'

'Fairly often.'

That's it then. I had better start praying that his parents don't pay another call on my parents, because this time there will be bloodshed.

'So now what?' I said.

Arun was busy screwing up his face and looking into the sky.

'Arun, did you hear me?'

'I was wondering if clouds could overpower the sun.'

'What?'

'I mean, it's such a lovely day, the sun seems so strong and powerful in the sky. If any clouds came along, who would be the stronger, the sun or them? Could all this lovely sunshine disappear and be replaced by rain?'

I was getting riled by now. 'Listen, your preoccupation with whimsical observation is completely lost on me.' I pointed to myself to emphasise my point.

'Ohh, big words, for a young girl.' He smiled at me.

I didn't smile back. 'Arun, listen to me, I'm worried.'

He pulled me into his arms and kissed me. 'Rell, don't fret, don't worry. Our relationship will stand the test of time. That's why I was wondering about the sun and the rain. That's us. We're the sun and everybody else is the

113

rain. As long as we keep shining, no one can affect us.'

How could I answer that? Arun's arms encircled me, but I didn't feel the security I needed. Inside fear, anxiety and worry were jostling for first place in my heart. It might not have been raining outside, but it sure felt like it inside. I wished I could have shared his optimism, but meeting that woman and Priya of all people had just knocked that out of me with one almighty swipe. Whooooosh. Gone.

'Have you enjoyed yourself?'

I nodded. It had been a good day, even though it didn't start off too brilliantly. In the end, we had managed to put our worries behind us.

As we approached the car, laughing and joking with each other, I was suddenly aware that Arun had tensed up. He had stopped walking.

Pulling his arm, I tried to drag him along. I thought he was teasing me. 'C'mon, Arun, stop messing about.'

He only stared ahead. When I looked to see what he was looking at, what I saw made me stop too.

By the car were three Asian men. Two were about thirty-something and one was much older.

A feeling of dizziness overcame me. I wanted to blank out completely. My mouth was dry and my legs were threatening to give way. There was nowhere to run; nothing but grass and trees surrounded us. Not a soul was in sight, even though there were a few cars parked nearby. No one.

The older man took a step forward and said something I couldn't understand to Arun. He nodded his head towards me.

Arun kept his mouth shut.

The man spoke even loader, and this time he pointed his finger at me. Arun said something back to him which seemed to strike an unpleasant chord in the man, because he rushed at Arun, taking everyone by surprise, and slapped him across the face. Then, as the two other men quickly came to the older man's side, one of them said, 'All right, Dad, leave it out.'

Arun and the older man, who by now I realised was his dad, stared each other out. There was more talking going on between the three of them, and just as I was feeling as though I was invisible, one of the younger men said to me, 'Come, we'll take you home.'

Arun said, 'No, I'll take her home.'

More words were spoken and then Arun said, 'Come on, Rell, I'm taking you home.'

We climbed into the car, with the voice of his dad ringing in our ears. One of the younger men got into the back of our car.

As Arun turned round, the guy started talking in Punjabi. Turning to face him I said, 'Do you mind? I am alive, you know.' How I managed to speak I don't know, but I was very glad I did, because he looked taken aback, found his manners and apologised.

Then he started talking to me, as a person of understanding!

'I'm Arun's elder brother, my name is Sunil. The thing is, our family is very close and I'm sure, like your family, we want what is best for each other. Now, Arun has already been spoken to about your relationship and it is clear he is not listening.'

My negative feelings towards Sunil were being replaced with feelings of self-preservation and pride. 'So, eh, Sunil, first tell me what has been said about me, and then tell me what you mean about wanting the best for each other.'

Arun kept quiet.

'Well . . . um . . . sorry, what's your name again?'

'Sorrelle.'

'It's like this, Sorrelle.' He was very blunt. 'You're black and we are Asian. Everything about us is different. So what future is there going to be for you and my brother? None. My parents want him to disassociate himself from you . . .'

'Disassociate himself from me! Do you think I have a disease or something? Let me tell you something, my parents are not too happy about this relationship either. But I happen to think that Asian people and black people should stick together. What is your family worried about exactly? What do you think will happen if we continue our relationship?'

Sunil paused and looked at me. 'Sorrelle, you seem like a nice girl. You seem bright and intelligent. But the bottom line is this: my family is well known and respected in our community. Our community is important to us and we want to maintain it and protect it. Arun must do well in all areas of his life and his successes must benefit his people.'

As we drove along, the countryside was fast disappearing. Grey town buildings were more and more frequent. I didn't entirely understand Sunil, but I knew broadly where this conversation was going. What was the point in my trying to reason with Arun's brother about our relationship? We could go on and on and still end up where we first started.

'. . . so, you see, if you finished it now, you could go back to living normal lives.'

'And if we don't?'

He shrugged.

I didn't want to look at Arun. 'Drop me off at the station,' I said. I couldn't risk him dropping me off at home. Another showdown – this time with my parents – would be too much.

I opened the car door and Arun and I just looked at each other. His brother got into the seat that I had just vacated, and I wanted to say something stinging – like, aren't you afraid of catching something – but I thought it was best to keep my mouth shut.

When I got home, no one was in. It was very quiet. I wished I could talk to someone about it – even Priya. She could explain Asian ways and customs, then I might have an understanding of what I was up against. But how could I trust her? And then I thought, how did Arun's dad know exactly where to find us?

The house seemed hollow and unfriendly. I wanted to know what was happening to Arun. He hadn't really resisted his family, in fact he had acted more like a lamb going to be slaughtered. I had heard stories about Asian girls being locked in their rooms, their clothes being taken away and things like that. Was that what was going to happen to Arun? I was itching to phone him. I thought it best to get out of the house.

***

Aunt Melda's remedy for pain was – food.

I don't know how I found myself at her house. It was as though my feet knew where to go and my body just followed on.

I told her the whole sorry tale about me and Arun, in much more detail than I had before, and I told her what had happened today.

'. . . What me can't understand is how dem found out where yu's were. When dem sey Arun must drive a certain car dem did do something to it, so dat dem could easily trace it.'

This made me feel a little better, but I told Aunt Melda she was being a bit far-fetched.

'Yu tink so? People with money can do what dem like, believe me.'

'So, Aunt Melda, what do I do now?'

'Chile, yu is not going fi take me advice, so don't ask me.'

'No, c'mon, tell me what you think?'

'Well, dis is young love. Yu will surprise yurself in how yu get over it. Don't get me wrong, yu will never forget it, but de pain will lighten up. But knowing yu and young people generally, yu will want to fight to de death. Me only hope sey it is quick, cause de holiday in Florida will help yu get over it.'

I thought about what she said. I didn't want to break up with Arun. Something inside me was urging me on to keep at the relationship. The only thing I wanted to break with was Arun's family. Then again, if I was honest, I was feeling a bit let down by Arun. He hadn't really stuck up for me with his dad and his brothers. And in the car, he'd just let Sunil do all the talking. And yet . . . I'd got closer to him than I had to any other guy. It was all so confusing.

'Oh I don't know, Aunt Melda. I'm so mixed up by the whole thing. His family have been so determined to get me out of their lives. They must think they are something really special.'

'Yes, well, dem must realise we is all flesh and blood. Some have riches, some don't. Some have good looks, some don't. De is always an opposite side to any situation.'

Then a horrible thought struck me. I wondered if Arun's parents had visited my home.

'Can I use your phone, Aunt Melda?'

'Sure.'

Trenton answered. 'What do you want?'

'I just wanted to know if someone was home.'

'Yeah, me. Where are you?'

'At Aunt Melda's.'

'When you coming home?'

'Soon.'

'Shall I pick you up?'

I sighed. This short conversation with Trenton was making me feel as if I had just done ten rounds with Lennox Lewis.

'I'll see you, Trent.' I put the phone down.

Standing at the bus stop, I contemplated walking home. The evening was cool, and I wanted to think.

'I love him, I love him not. I love him, I love him not.' The sentence kept revolving round and round in my mind. I was beginning to feel a bit less euphoric about

119

Arun. On the other hand, I still felt something strong for him. It was difficult to work it all out on my own. Normal situations I could cope with, but this was a little too complex for me. 'Shall I just talk to Mum about it?' I said aloud, and a man at the bus stop looked at me strangely.

A car pulled up and a familiar voice said, 'Are you off home? Hop in, I'll give you a lift.'

Would you believe it? It was Priya, in a cab.

'Thanks.'

She looked at me. 'You all right?'

Tears from nowhere pricked my eyes and I had to get a grip on myself.

'Um, look, mate, forget about taking me home, drop us up by the zebra crossing.' The cab driver did as Priya said and then she leaned across me, opened the door and said, 'Come on, Rell, let's go and sit in Moben's for a while.'

I didn't resist.

Sipping fizzy mango juice, while Priya tucked into a samosa, I reluctantly began to talk to her. The most important thing was to get her to promise me that she wouldn't tell anyone what I said, especially her family.

'I'm stupidly trusting you, Priya. If you let me down I don't know what I'll end up doing.'

'No, honestly, Rell. I won't breathe a word.' We looked into each other's eyes and I was hoping that she would keep her mouth shut.

'I just want to say, Rell, that I didn't think my dad would tell Arun's dad like that. I only found out after he told him and to be truthful I didn't think of it as anything important.' She shrugged her shoulders. 'But then, when

120

we had that fight, I spoke to my mum and she told me that Arun's parents were going mental that he was going out with a black girl. She told me that I should keep right out of it. I honestly didn't want to cause you all this trouble. I know you'll find it hard to believe, because I acted jealous when you and Arun started going out together, but I never intended to cause problems for you.'

'Well, you're right about one thing. They're certainly going mental. I think they *are* mental! We're only dating, for goodness' sake, you would think we were going to elope or something! Nothing like that is happening. Why can't they leave us alone?'

'It's all to do with tradition, Rell. You do realise that if they thought that your relationship was heavy, and babies or marriage were on the cards, they would cut him off.' Her hand slashed through the air.

I couldn't help smiling at her melodramatic gesture. It was typical Priya. And I believed her when she said she hadn't really wanted to cause me trouble. Perhaps we could stay friends after all.

'What do you think will happen now, Rell?'

'To be truthful, I don't know, Priya. I only hope it doesn't get worse.'

Eleven

It was the worst night of my life. I had a nightmare. I dreamt I was walking along a beach with Arun, laughing and joking. The waves were gently flowing in and out, and then suddenly a giant freak wave came in and lifted us both up and – whoosh – it disappeared out to sea, taking Arun with it. I was left on beach alone. I began to run towards Arun but the wave was a powerful one and it took him miles away. To make matters worse, there were sharks and other strange predatory creatures all around, snapping at me. It was just impossible. I was screaming and crying, it was too dreadful. When I woke up, I was drenched in sweat.

Since the day Arun got carted off by his dad and brothers I had not seen or heard from him. I had tried to phone him on his mobile, but it was switched off. I hadn't been able to contact him for three days and I was getting frantic. At least Priya and I were talking again. I was pleased about that. Our relationship had changed, but we were still friends. I asked her to see what she could find out about Arun, but so far she hadn't come back to me with anything. I even asked Zara if she could find out anything through Trenton, but she drew a blank too.

The day after my nightmare, I was really hoping Arun would come to Sainsbury's to see me, but there was no sign of him. Instead I had Irene talking incessantly in my ear.

'How comes you're not your usual perky self, Sorrelle?' She enquired as she plonked herself next me in the staff room. She was the last person I wanted to speak to but, being a bit thick, she would start plying me with questions if I told her I didn't want to talk.

'Oh, I've just got a few things on my mind.'

'Not that Indian bloke you were seeing? Nothing but aggravation, men are. It doesn't matter what colour, class or cute package they come in, it boils down to the same thing.'

I sort of gave her a grin and looked down at the floor. She isn't easily put off.

'I've got a friend who went out with a black bloke once, she had all sorts of trouble. He had a string of girlfriends, and he used to take her money, and on top of that her parents didn't like him, and his girlfriend – the one that he was living with – didn't like her. It was a right carry-on. I told her to leave him, but she came out with all this claptrap about how much she loved him. Anyway, I think he left her for someone else. I said it would all end in tears, but she wasn't listening.'

I was trying not to either.

'So, have you met his parents yet?'

I couldn't stand her any longer. 'Irene, why don't you do me a big favour and shut up!'

'No need to bite my head off! Has he packed you up then?'

I got up and walked off. Locking myself in the toilet cubicle, I broke down and cried, silently so that no one could hear me. The thought of going back on the checkout was making me feel worse and I decided there and then to go off sick. But first, I let the tears flow as my mind jumped from one awful scene to another.

Had his parents packed him off to India?

Was he going to be forced into a marriage that he didn't want?

Were his parents holding him against his will?

My head felt like a revolving door that was out of control. My body was weak, which was understandable since I had hardly eaten since Wednesday. Mum kept looking at me suspiciously. She had asked on a few occasions if I was okay, but I just told her I was fine.

If only Arun would contact me to let me know that he was all right. It was the not knowing that was doing my head in.

I washed my face. There were only hard, green paper towels and it felt like someone was trying to claw my face as I used a couple to dry myself. Taking a deep breath, I went in search of my supervisor to tell her I didn't feel well. It was true, I did feel ill, and continuing to work would be detrimental to my health.

As I got to the top of the road, I thought my eyes were

playing tricks on me. There, in the flesh, was a haggard-looking Arun. I screwed up my eyes. I had to look real hard to make sure it was him.

'Arun!' I called.

He smiled and started walking towards me.

'Rell!' He hugged and kissed me. 'Am I glad to see you! I was trying to figure out a way to see you, but I didn't want to disturb you while you were working. On the other hand, I didn't want to be hanging around out here until you finished either. How come you've left work early?'

'I couldn't stand it any longer, I had to get out of that place. But what's happened to you. Where have you been? Why didn't you contact me? I've been sick with worry.'

He glanced around and then he took my hand. 'Where can we go, Rell, where we can have a bit of privacy?'

I said the first name that came into my head. 'Aunt Melda's.'

I phoned her from a call box and she told me to bring Arun to her house. On the bus, I could sense that Arun was tense. He kept squeezing my hand every now and then, but he wasn't really saying much. I didn't press him, but I had an idea that his parents must have confiscated his phone and his car.

Briefing Arun about Aunt Melda prepared him.

'Hello, young man, yu is de one who stop Rell from coming to Florida with me, hmm?'

'I, um, well . . .' He grinned at her.

'Don't bother to tell me any lie, me can see yu have a cheeky face. Come in den, an me will fix yu something to eat.'

She had made rice with ackee and saltfish.

'This is lovely food, Aunt Melda, you're a good cook,' Arun said.

My appetite had not returned and I still couldn't eat, but watching Arun tuck in, and being near to him, made me feel a lot better.

'There's so much fi me to do still, with me packing an such, so me will have to excuse meself fi a lickle while, okay? Yu all right now, Roonie?'

'I'm fine, and thanks, Aunt Melda, I really do appreciate what you're doing for us.'

Smiling, Aunt Melda said, 'Oh, it's nothing.' Looking at me, she nodded her head towards the door. 'Come, Rell, me want fi show yu something. Me won't keep her a second.'

I followed Aunt Melda down the hallway and she beckoned me to come upstairs. Once we arrived in her bedroom she said, 'Listen, chile, me don't mind helping yu out at a bad time, but yu know me is gwan have fi tell yur mother.'

'But Aunt . . .'

'Hold on. What yu don't know is that yur mother has already come to me for advice on what to do about you and him.' She pointed towards the floor, indicating Arun downstairs. 'If yur mother find out sey me a harbour yu and him, an me did not tell her, she will be very upset with me an rightly so.'

'But why, Aunt Melda? What she doesn't know won't hurt her.'

'Hurt her, me will tell yu what is hurting her. Yu. She used to boast sey yu is a model daughter an how yu can talk bout anyting, yu come in like sisters. Dat was before yu did hitch up with Roonie.'

'Really?' This was the first time I was hearing this and it wasn't making me feel too good.

'Now yur mother thinks that she is a failure. Yur father is blaming yur mother for everyting, an as far as he is concern de day yu tell dem dat yu is going fi have dat bwoy picknee is de day yur father sey his is gwine fling yu out of him house.'

'Oh no, I told Mum that I wasn't sleeping with Arun, and I'm not! Why doesn't she believe me?'

'Apparently, yu are not suppose to be seeing dis bwoy but yu are. So how can yur parents believe anyting yu sey, eh?'

'So why are you having us in your house then?' I said, sort of accusingly because I felt hurt at what she had just told me.

Aunt Melda didn't answer for a while, then she said, 'Chile, when yu have been on dis earth fi some time, yu come to understand a lot of tings. An yur situation is not a new situation, an it will keep on happening until Jesus come back. Me reason out dat it is better to bring out everyting inna de open, so we can see what an what is what. Dis secret, secret business cause too many problems, cos nobody is sure what is going on.'

I had to agree with her, but now I was going to have to face my mum. On the one hand, it was a good thing to be able to level with her and get it off my chest, but on the other, having to admit to her that I'd deceived her was going to be hard.

'Yu had better stop daydreaming and get back to yur young man.'

★★★

As we sat together on Aunt Melda's lumpy sofa with a million cushions all over the place, Arun began to fill me in on the events of the last few days.

'. . . When I got home, my dad was livid. To be truthful, I have never seen him so mad. I thought he was going to have a heart attack. My mum was crying, my granny was wailing, my brothers were saying I was a fool, my sisters-in-law were joining in. Even my younger sister and my nieces and nephew kept whispering, 'You're in big trouble, Uncle.' We both laughed at that. 'Out of respect, I stayed at home for a few days. My dad called my aunts and uncles and our family in India about me.'

'But, Arun, what is the big deal? Okay, so I'm black . . .'

'That is the main issue, but also I have disobeyed my parents, and that is considered very bad. My parents have high hopes for me. They want to have a big hand in my choice of a wife, and they want me to make a match within my community. I should be thinking of marriage now and they want me to start paying my attentions to an eligible Asian girl.'

'So what's go to happen now?'

'Well, my parents have taken my phone, I can't use any of the cars, my money has been restricted . . .'

'Which leaves you with zilch.'

He sat staring into space for a while, then, looking at me, he said softly, 'Don't you want to see me any more?'

'Don't be silly,' I said. And then I realised how his mind was working. 'Arun! It was not your money that attracted me to you! It's you I'm interested in, not your cars and your wallet!'

Arun held me close to him. I closed my eyes. Now was

the time, I thought. I had to face my parents – well, my mum at least – and whatever happened then, I'd have to deal with it.

Twelve

'What I'm finding hard to take in all of this is the fact that you have lied and cheated and behaved so out of character, Rell.' Mum was really upset.

Quietly I said, 'The thing is, Mum, I didn't feel that I was able to talk to you about it. After Arun's parents came round you weren't prepared to listen to what I had to say.'

'How can I believe anything you tell me now?'

We were talking at cross-purposes. The evening was warm and still, yet inside it was hot and tempers were threatening to torpedo out of control. Mum was stalking up and down the living room. She seemed to talk more to herself than to me.

'Your father was right.'

'Right about what?'

'That you can't be trusted.'

This was ridiculous. Most of the time, or I should say

all of the time, I have been straight down the line with Mum, but this one exception has knocked everything else out. I let Mum wear herself out stalking and shouting and then I went to my room.

Where was this all going to end? Arun and I wanted to keep seeing each other, but how it was going to happen I didn't know.

When we'd left Aunt Melda's, we'd stood gloomily at the bus stop. Not having a car was depressing Arun more and more by the minute. Then, by the time the bus arrived, it was nearly full and we had to stand up. It didn't bother me, but Arun was muttering and looking round angrily at the people sitting down. He'd wanted to take a cab home, doing a detour to drop me off, but he didn't have much money, so that was out.

He'd never been in this position before, but he seemed prepared to put up with it. Our relationship must have been important to him. I asked him if he felt sure he wanted to go on with this and he said, 'I have never been so sure of anything in my entire life.'

That did it for me.

My imagination ran riot. Before I knew it, I was picturing myself in a television studio with Oprah Winfrey, discussing mixed marriages!

'So, Sorrelle, how is life with you?' Oprah asked. 'By the way, I must say that Sorrelle is such a beautiful name.'

Smiling and showing off my Colgate-coated teeth, I waxed lyrical about how being married to Arun was bliss, and how cute having mixed-race children was wonderful too. In fact everything was wonderful.

'What about your in-laws?'

Hmm. That question would wipe the smile off my face. I'd have to explain that Arun was 'dead' to his family and so were my children. But what was I thinking? Marriage! We'd hardly got to know each other yet!

Our relationship still had a bit of an unreal feel to it for me, because I hadn't fully worked out in my mind why I was so keen on pursuing it. Did I love Arun? Or was I just being stubborn and clinging on to something I had been told I couldn't have? My whole life had changed. I had lied to my mother, hit my best friend – I had moved far away from the Sorrelle I thought I knew.

I heard Dad's voice and I knew that Mum must've found the courage to tell him. I heard a roar and the living-room door slam.

The best thing for me, I thought, is to go to bed. It was coming up to midnight and I was worn out.

No sooner had I got my head down than my door opened and Dad called my name. I was going to pretend that I was sleeping but the tone of his voice made me sit up.

'Yes, Dad.'

He came into the room and stood in front of me. Mum was nowhere in sight. He was not smiling.

'Sorrelle, your mother has just been telling me about you and this boy.' Dad wasn't too happy saying his name. 'Let me tell you this, seeing how little respect you have for yourself . . .'

'Dad, that's not true . . .'

'What have I told you about interrupting me? Now, what I mean is this. This boy's family came round to my house and made it very plain that they did not want their son to go out with a black girl; they got that message across very clear. I told them how I stood as well, and it was generally accepted that you would both not see each other.'

I began to feel that I was one of Dad's pupils sitting in the classroom. All he needed was a blackboard and some chalk.

'But for some time your mother and I have suspected that you have been defying us. Now you have admitted it. I just want to say this: don't get yourself pregnant.'

'Dad, that's the last thing I want to do!'

'Do you think you're the only young girl that has said that? Thousands and millions of young girls think they can handle boys, but in fact they can't and then they expect their parents to pick up the pieces! Well, let me tell you, not this parent!'

I rolled my eyes and crossed my arms. I couldn't be bothered to argue with Dad. When he had made up his mind about something, that was it.

'You'll end up living in a high-rise council flat on some estate . . .'

'Dad, Dad, will you listen to me? I don't intend to get pregnant, and besides, is that all you're concerned about? Don't you care about how I feel about Arun and how he feels about me? I have to experience life for myself and find things out for myself! I'm not stupid, you know. I do hear stories and watch TV and read books. I don't think I'm better or cleverer than any other girl, but I don't want to throw my life down the drain because of Arun or any man! No one's talking about children or marriage or

133

anything like that!'

Dad gave a dry laugh. 'Brave words, Rell, but what will you say when things don't work out how you thought they would? I know what young men have on their minds and that leads to children, believe you me!'

What was the point in discussing this with Dad? We were just going round in circles. He was getting more and more irate. I suspected a full-blown row was on the cards. I was right.

'. . . His family are probably calling you all kinds of names right now – like black whore and . . .'

'Who cares? I know what I am and what other people think of me. I just don't care about being called names!'

By now I was out of bed with my hands on my hips. Dad had loosened his shirt and was sweating with anger.

'I care, your mother cares, your brother cares, but you say you don't care. You should be ashamed of yourself.'

'Ashamed? What for? I haven't done anything.'

Mum burst into the room.

'Okay, you two, this isn't going to solve anything.'

But that didn't stop me and Dad going for each other. By the time Dad left the room I was crying, something I hadn't done for ages, until I started going out with Arun. Now it seemed that I was bawling my eyes out every day. It was hot and sticky and I had to open the window to let in some fresh air. It didn't let in much, but it made me breathe a little more easily. I was thirsty too, but I didn't want to see Dad again for the night so I stayed in my room.

Why was everyone so upset about me and Arun? It was like a strange mystery that was hard to unravel. If I was pregnant or something really bad was happening, yes, I could understand all this concern. But we had only just started going out with each other and it was like World War III had broken out. I was having to ask myself, is this all worth it? Should I just call it a day and forget the whole thing?

I knew the answer to that – no.

Why should people tell me how to live my life? I had to find out what I wanted and make my own decisions. I just knew that if I started to change to please other people, it would backfire on me and I would be the one who would end up unhappy.

The funny thing was, Dad was forever saying 'be yourself', and here I was taking his advice to the max and he didn't like it. My rebellious streak was really coming out, and, to be honest, that was what was keeping me hanging on.

All of a sudden, I felt stronger and more determined. I really liked Arun and I was definitely going to stick to my guns.

Nothing gonna split us up.

Thirteen

'Look on the bright side, Arun, at least it's still summer.'

'Big deal. You don't understand how I feel. It's bad enough taking buses everywhere, but to have to meet my girlfriend in the park, it's rubbish.'

I was trying my hardest to get Arun to see that it was no problem to meet up in Valentine's Park. It's a nice place and it's so big you can find a spot where no one will bother you. But it was bothering Arun.

If he had a car, any car, and if he had money – we wouldn't be sitting in the park!

It was funny how things seemed to have reversed. At home, it was now generally accepted that I was going out with Arun. Nothing much was said, but when I said I was off out, I didn't get interrogated. My shouting match with Dad had been awful, but it had cleared the air. Even if he didn't like the situation, he wasn't trying to stop me seeing Arun any more. I think Mum must have had a quiet word with him. She and I had had a calmer conversation the next day, and we'd sort of made up.

But my relationship with Arun was going through a down period. I knew that it was because his parents had taken away his money and he couldn't drive a car, but as far as I was concerned we had each other and that was the main thing.

Arun didn't see it like that,

'Part of the joy in taking a girl out is being able to treat her to meals and clothes . . .'

'So you're saying that it's no longer a joy to be with me?'

'No, I'm not saying that . . .'

'So what are you saying?'

He folded his arms and pouted. Looking at him, I thought, 'What a big kid!' His parents have stung him where it hurts and he can't deal with it.

I tried to put my arm around him, but he pushed me off.

Hurt by his rejection, I said, 'This is no good, Arun. You were the one who wanted to know if I would still be interested in you if you didn't have any money, and now you haven't you're blanking me. You've got to stop it. Now we have a chance to get our lives on the road, you're in danger of mashing it up!'

Grudgingly (or so I thought), he put his arm around me.

'Rell, I can't explain to you how I am feeling. I'm angry with my parents for doing this to me. This is blackmail. All I am doing is dating you, but you would think I was planning a bank robbery or something. At home nobody is talking to me, which is uncomfortable, but I can handle that. But the rest – it's hard to explain.'

'So what are you saying, you want to knock it on the head?'

Quickly he said, 'No no, not at all. It's just,' he sighed, 'it's just . . . oh, I don't know.'

Sitting on the grass with our backs to a large tree, we both got lost in our individual thoughts. I didn't want to think like this, but Arun was making me. Here I was, out of sorts with my family, fighting off my friends, cancelling a holiday to Florida, and Arun was worrying about stupidness. I was trying to blank all the hassle out, because this relationship had cost too much already and I wanted to get some return from it.

'Come on, let's go for a walk, Rell.'

We strolled through the park, Arun's arm around my shoulders. The beautiful flowers lifted my spirits and they seemed to do the same for Arun. He squeezed my shoulder and then kissed me on the cheek.

'You know something? You're beautiful,' he said. 'And I don't care what anyone does as long as we can be together.'

My heart did a somersault and landed in my toes.

'Me too,' was all I could say.

'Come on, let me get you an ice cream.'

For the rest of the day we walked in the park and then we sat in McDonald's in Cranbrook Road. Arun walked me home from Ilford. By the time I got in I had to have a bath with some of that muscle-soothing stuff. My legs were aching and it felt as though someone had kicked me in the back. This must be what it's like to be middle-aged and unfit.

We tried to see each other as much as possible but, living so far apart with no car, it was proving difficult. That was unfortunate, but at least we didn't have the hassle of lying to our parents and having to sneak about and be in fear of being found out. I thought that our relationship might now be going in the right direction.

Mum and I were friends again and she asked me if I wanted to come up the West End with her. I jumped at the chance.

On the train, Mum started telling me about Sister Pauline's son, who was going off the rails.

'. . . She can't understand why he's behaving like that. But I told her, she has to let him make his own decisions, isn't that true?' She looked at me. I nodded. Then she said, 'How are you and Arun?'

'Great.'

'I would like to meet him, you know, but if he comes to the house, your father will go mad. I keep telling him you're both going out with each other, you're of an age where you have to make your own decisions to find out about life, but he won't listen to me.'

Mum sounded like a typical social worker who is working on a case. I was glad that she had come to the conclusion that she had to let me get on with it. I don't know what would have happened if my parents had insisted that I couldn't see Arun. Would I have run away? Disobeyed them anyway? It sounded so drastic now, but all those thoughts did go through my mind. When feelings are running high, rational thinking takes a dive out the window.

'You'll like him, Mum.'

'I'm sure I will. I suppose I should have accepted this sooner. I think his parents coming round like that and the shock of it all overwhelmed me. I mean, he's a young man, surely his parents should let him do what he wants? But then the Asian culture places such a strong emphasis on what the community thinks.'

'Tell me about it.'

'But, Rell, you dad thinks they rejected you because you were black – because you weren't good enough for them. That's what is eating into him. After all, Asian people go through the same racial abuse that we black people do. You would think they would be sensitive to how we would feel.'

'But Mum, some Asian people identify with black people and some of them don't. That's not Arun's fault. He doesn't think he's too good for me!'

Mum sighed. 'Yes, and we're all encouraged to be at each other's throats. After all, while we're arguing with Arun's family we're forgetting who's really responsible for racism.'

I looked at her, puzzled. She smiled. 'You know, every time there's a really bad example of racism that hits the news, some tabloid will run a feature on how black and Asian people are at each other's throats. We're all racists, too, that's what they suggest, so we shouldn't complain about racism against *us*.'

The train pulled into Bond Street Station. Mum hit Marks & Spencer with a vengeance. Apparently, this was the biggest M&S in London. I was grateful for all the walking I'd been doing with Arun, because I was in some kind of decent shape to keep up with Mum. We must have looked at every item of clothing they had in the store, then Mum tried on just about all of it, and it wasn't until she felt not hungry, but ravenous, that she stopped.

As we munched our sandwiches and walked towards Oxford Circus, I had such a feeling of peace inside. Even though my feet were killing me and I felt sticky and grimy, I was with my mum. I wondered, if Mum hadn't come round would I have given up Arun to be friends with Mum or have given up Mum to be Arun's girl-friend? I'm glad I didn't have to make that choice.

The only thing that did mar the day happened on the train home when Mum asked me if I was still going to Florida.

'Oh, I don't know', I said, 'I don't really think I can go. I've messed Aunt Melda around so much. I can't really change my mind again.'

'She won't mind. It would be better to go so she doesn't lose her money, which you would have to repay. But if you do go, it's a gift. I do think you'd be mad to turn down such a lovely holiday.'

To be honest, thoughts of Florida had been drifting in and out of my mind. I wouldn't mind going. But the timing was all wrong. It would be fine if the trip was months away and my relationship with Arun had been firmly established. But right now we were still in the early stages, like a child trying to walk on its own without the balance right yet or the strength in its legs to stand alone. If I went now, would I have something to come back to?

I didn't or couldn't answer Mum's question. This Florida business was still a thorny subject. I thought it best to let it drop.

'What, on Saturday?'

Priya didn't want to answer me.

'C'mon, tell me, is the party this Saturday?'

Sighing, she said, 'Yes.'

'I'm glad you told me, Priya. Don't worry, I won't jump on you, it's just that Arun never told me anything.' I tried to make it sound light and casual, but inside I was fuming.

Priya was sitting at the end of my bed with her back against the wall. 'Anyway, Rell, I'm not buying anything new.'

'That's a surprise, you've got so much stuff anyway.' I was still seething, but I didn't want Priya to know it was bothering me.

Apparently, on Saturday – the next day – Amarjit, Arun's cousin, was having a party for his birthday, and loads of people had been invited. But not me – unless Arun was planning to tell me on the day, and he just hadn't said anything up to now. I wasn't mad with Priya. She'd assumed that I knew and was going. But I was furious with Arun. What was his game? Even if his family were going to be there, they knew we were still seeing each other, so why the secrecy? It was like the wedding all over again. I'd decided not to go to that – it wasn't worth the hassle – and I'd stopped worrying about it, but now Arun was excluding me again! I had to put it out of my mind. I would explode otherwise.

'. . .You're not listening to me, Rell.'

'Oh, I'm sorry, Priya, what were you saying?'

'That I'm going out with Flavour.'

'But he's black!' I shouted in shock.

'Yeah, and he's tasty.'

Flavour was ebony black, and good-looking, and he knew it. But – Priya and him?

'What will your parents say?'

'What the eye can't see the heart can't grieve over.'

'You're playing with fire.'

Grinning, she said, 'He is gorgeous. He said to me the other day, "The darker the berry, the sweeter the juice." Isn't that sexy?'

I thought it was slack. I couldn't even bring myself to ask her if she had slept with him. I didn't want to know. One thing I did know was that if her parents ever found out that she was going out with a black man, they would throw her out of the house.

'So you're copying me then?'

'No, I'm just having some fun.'

'I thought you liked Kamal?'

'I do, but he hasn't asked me out, so I thought Flavour and I could spend some quality time together. What do you think?'

'I think you'd better be careful that you don't get burnt.'

By the time Priya went home her exuberant mood had rubbed me up the wrong way. That she could enter this relationship so easily after all my troubles did seem unfair. But, really, I wished them well. I couldn't wait to see Arun. As I stood in the kitchen thinking about it, the phone rang and it was him. It would have been better to have spoken to him face to face, but I couldn't wait for that. I let him talk about nothing in particular for a while and then, trying to be cool and laid-back, I asked him what we were doing tomorrow.

'Um . . . you're working tomorrow.'

'I meant in the evening. There's a film I wouldn't mind seeing. It's at Gants Hill, which is nice and convenient.'

'I've not got that much cash, Rell.'

'It doesn't matter. I'll pay.'

'No way. You're my woman . . .'

'Don't call me your woman, it sounds . . .'

'Okay, okay, you're my girl and I don't want to get into the habit of letting you pay for both of us.'

'So what shall we do?' I was gritting my teeth by now. I could sense that he was being evasive and I knew why.

'I don't know. Maybe we might have to give Saturday a miss. We can meet up in the park on Sunday.'

'But the weather's been rubbish. What will we do if it's raining? Meet up on Monday?' I knew I was being sarcastic but he was beginning to bring the worst out in me.

I didn't want to talk to him.

'I've got to go now, Arun. Look, phone me tomorrow and maybe we will have come up with something.'

He didn't say anything at first. I could tell that his mind was ticking over. He was probably trying to decide if he should tell me or not.

He didn't.

'Speak to you tomorrow then, Rell.'

'Yeah.'

'I miss you,' he whispered.

144

'Yeah, bye.' I put the phone down.

I was quietly raging. The fact that I had to do it almost silently made the raging even worse. After all that we had been through, he was holding out on me. To make matters worse, while I was still in the kitchen Trenton and Zara came in. They were messing about like young lovers do, which annoyed me no end, and then Zara said, 'Are you all set for the hottest party in town tomorrow?'

I nearly choked on my glass of water. They were going!

'Yeah,' I said feebly. It was hard to get any words out.

Zara, looking concerned, said, 'Are you all right?'

I just nodded. I wanted to get out of the kitchen fast. She must have signalled to Trenton, because he slipped out the door.

'What's up, Rell?'

'Am I that transparent?'

Zara laughed and said yes.

Sitting down at the table, I told her about Arun not mentioning the party.

'What's the guy playing at? Look at all the trouble you've both been through! Perhaps his parents are going to be there?'

'Ple-asss-e!' I said, with one eyebrow raised.

'Well, it was a thought. You don't think . . .'

I finished off the sentence for her – 'He's got someone else? No.' And I didn't. Arun wasn't a two-timing, scheming pig. He was something else that I hadn't found the right name for yet.

'Why don't you still go then?'

'What, by myself?'

'No, come with us.'

'Trent's not going to like that.'

'But if you say that you want to come with us because Arun hasn't got a car and you don't want to go by bus, he won't mind.'

It took me a second to make up my mind. 'I'm coming.'

I kept trying to come up with the reason why Arun hadn't told me. It went round and round in my mind. It was like an unquenchable fire that wouldn't go out. I would have to wait for Saturday night to find out the answer.

Would our relationship stand it?

Fourteen

'This is like a cold winter's day,' said Mum. 'I was planning on doing some gardening, but it'll be all mud and slush out there.'

'Forget it, Mum,' said Trenton as he crammed his face with toast and jam. 'You'll have to leave it for a couple of weeks until the ground gets a bit more hard.'

'Thanks for your advice, son, perhaps we'll both do some gardening.'

The handful of cornflakes in my bowl had turned soggy. I couldn't face them.

'Rell can help you. She loves gardening.'

'Leave Rell out of this. This is why I had a big, strong, strapping son, to help me do the heavy work.'

'That's sexist, Mum!'

'Wash the breakfast things for me then, Trent?'

Trenton quickly made an exit, but not before grabbing

147

two bananas and a handful of grapes to accompany the three slices of toast he'd already had.

Laughing at him, Mum said, 'That boy is too much.'

But I was not really taking it in. The rain slashed down with a vengeance. The day was dark and dismal. It looked just like I felt.

My mind was stuck in a groove. I wished that I could have a break from it, so that I could have some rest. It was torture.

Arun.

Why couldn't I just think about him now and again, instead of all the time? It was constant, like a nagging pain that wouldn't go away. It seemed that I had been going out with him all my life, and not just a few weeks. How could so much happen in such a short time?

Was this love — the joy and the pain? Right now I wouldn't mind giving the pain bit a miss!

The thought of going to work nauseated me. I had to go though; I needed the money, since Arun hadn't got much now, and even though he got annoyed when I spent mine, what else were we supposed to do? I didn't mind, but I had made myself a mental note. In future, when I heard about girls spending money on their guys, I'd spare them my lecture on being stupid. Sometimes these situations couldn't be avoided.

The party.

I kept wondering whether or not I should go. I really didn't want to go, but I had to find out why Arun had failed to tell me about it. Already I had come up with at least a hundred different reasons — well, maybe not quite so many, but enough. My brain was throbbing with the stress that I'd put it through.

I remembered a story that Aunt Melda had told me about somebody she knew from her schooldays in Jamaica: 'Cornie was a part-way Chinese an part-way black man who loved women, an dem did love him. One in particular was my friend Eliza. When me tell yu dat she love him, she love him, she love him. Because him was a pretty bwoy his mother had high hopes for him an did want fi send him to the States. Him never like learning, only ramping.

'Den Eliza get catch, an did have a picknee, what a beautiful girl chile. An she down on him fi get married. From time me did warn her sey, "Cornie is not de marrying type so don't try no tricks." Did she listen? No. Everybody talk to her, but she did make up fi her mind. Yu know something, love is a weapon. It's more deadly dan any bomb. It can start off quietly an before yu know it − boooom.

'Well, Eliza was living inna dream world. All de time she was thinking, get picknee, get married, have a nice time together. An Cornie was thinking, have a good time with Eliza, when tings get rough, the rough get going. Him de gone pon a next woman. It did mess up poor Eliza brain. An like a bomb she explode. She turn mad. Clear crazy.'

At first when Aunt Melda told me this story I laughed, but now I could understand that emotions can run deep and if they're not dealt with − they can explode.

'Aren't you going to work, Rell. Look at the time, you'll be late.'

Slowly, I got up from the table. I was tired on account

of lack of sleep. I had been tossing and turning all night, thinking about – Arun.

Mum came up to me and placed both hands on my shoulders.

'Look at you, Rell. What's wrong?'

I wished I could tell Mum what was going on in my head, but I felt a bit foolish. I didn't want her telling me I told you so, and besides, I wanted to handle it myself.

By the time I got myself together and out the door, I was already five minutes late.

Twenty-five minutes later I was sitting at my till.

My body was in Sainsbury's but my mind was somewhere else. I had nearly convinced myself that Arun was seeing another girl, an Asian girl. When an Asian girl came to my till, I would look daggers at her, wondering, 'Are you the one?' It was ridiculous, but I couldn't seem to stop myself. It was as though I had stopped being me, and something else had started to live in me, in my mind to be exact. It was becoming a battle to think normally.

To add to my confusion, Arun and Amarjit came into the store with a girl in tow, heightening my already suspicious state.

Why, I thought to myself, did they have to come here? Amarjit saw me first and gave me his cocky wink. I flashed a .05 of a second smile – blink and you'll miss it. He nudged Arun, who waved. Then he walked over to me, bold as brass. The checkout next to me wasn't being used, so he came and stood next to me in the aisle.

'Hello, princess.' He was full of beans.

I wanted to deal with him there and then.

Leaning closer to me, he said, 'Am I allowed to kiss you?'

Before I found out about the party business I would have grinned and said something coy, but now I wanted to do something violent to him. Instead I smiled. It's one of the hardest things I've had to do. I was thankful that I had a line of customers which kept me occupied, as I didn't want to talk to him. He was totally unaware of my fury. I was still sort of hoping that he would tell me about the party.

'What's wrong with you? Have you got a cold coming or something?'

I muttered 'Or something.'

'What did you say?'

'Nothing.'

Amarjit came to my till with the girl. I wanted to tell him not to come to me, because I knew him and those were the rules, but I kept shtoom. I wanted to see what he was buying. It was all stuff you would eat at a party – crisps, nuts, sausage rolls, dips, different types of cheese – he had a trolley full of things.

'Hello, gorgeous,' he grinned.

I gave him a second brief smile.

'How's life?'

'Great. What's all this food? Having a party, are we?'

I caught the glance that he gave to Arun and started to fume. The girl, who must have thought the sun was gonna shine at some point today, had all her midriff hanging out. She started to say something, but Amarjit quickly blocked her.

This was bad. I just wanted them out of my sight.

'Come on, help me load up.'

The girl squeezed past Amarjit and he pinched her bottom. That answered one question – she was with Amarjit.

'£64.27 please.'

Amarjit pulled a bundle of notes out of his pocket and paid me.

Just before they all left, Arun quickly gave me a peck on the cheek. 'See you later, Rell.'

I nodded.

I felt sick, not at what he'd said but the way he'd said it, not horribly, but in a way that I knew was special to me.

In the staff room I wanted to sit on my own to try and sort what was happening in my head and in my heart. But it didn't help. My head was saying, 'He's a liar, he's no good, he's just stringing you along', and my heart was saying, 'He cares for you, he wants this to work as much as you do.' But the bottom line was, 'Why hasn't he told me about the party, still?' Arun just had the perfect opportunity to say something about it and he didn't say one word. Why the big mystery? As far as I was concerned, something must be up.

The girls on my break were having a big discussion about 'men'.

I didn't get involved, but I couldn't help overhearing. Someone was having man trouble and everybody was giving her advice.

I couldn't listen to it any more so I went into the loos.

Trying to work out my thoughts sitting on a loo seat was difficult. Abandoning that idea, I went back to work.

It was busy, which is great, because time seemed to speed up and before I knew it I was walking along Eastern Avenue on my way home. The rain had stopped, but the sun had gone on holiday. I suppose we all need a break!

As I opened the front door, Mum had just put the phone down.

'Oh Rell, that was Arun. I told him you weren't home yet.'

'Did he say he was going to ring back?'

Mum thought for a moment. 'I'm not sure.'

'What do you mean, "I'm not sure"? Did he say that or not?'

'What's wrong with you? I think he said that he'd see you later.'

That didn't mean a thing.

'Anyway, we had a little chat.' Mum smiled.

Alarm bells started ringing in my head. 'A little chat, about what?'

I followed Mum into the kitchen.

'Oh, about things.'

Mum was annoying me. 'About me?'

'Sort of, and other things.'

'Mum,' I sighed. This was too much.

'Well, I wanted to know what he was like, and I know it was only a short time on the phone . . .'

'What do you think?'

'I think he sounds like a nice boy, but – '

'But what?'

Looking at me, Mum seemed a bit sad. 'Put it this way, if it wasn't for all this palaver about his parents not liking you and all that, I wondered if you and he would still be seeing each other.'

'Yeah, of course we would.' I said it without even thinking.

In my room, I mulled over what Mum had said. Was it true? Was it because our parents were violently opposed to us being together, that we *were* still together? Although Mum had come around a bit, I didn't think she was really happy about the situation. But she was trying to be liberal and allow me to sort it through myself. I'm sure that if I asked for her advice, though, she would have loads to give me.

With my uniform still on, I lay on my bed. This was something I had never done before. Always, always, when we came home from wherever, our clothes had to be changed. It seemed like everything normal in my life had grown legs and run and now I didn't know where I was.

I could hear a loud knocking, as though someone was bashing inside my head.

It was Zara, hammering against my door.

It was dark outside and inside my room. I must have fallen asleep.

'What's the time?'

'A quarter to ten. Are you still coming?'

'Yeah, I can't believe the time. I must have gone out like a light.'

She came into the room and sat on my bed. 'You sure you're all right?'

I sat up and rubbed my eyes. 'Oh yeah, I'm fine. I just

want to get this thing sorted out. I can't stop thinking about it, and there's no way that I want all this confusion going on in my head. It's nearly giving me brain damage. And the thing is, Arun doesn't know any of this. It's me whose suffering, not him. This has got to stop.'

Zara stood up. 'Good for you, Rell. It's true, there's no point in torturing yourself. Get it sorted and get on with your life.'

Within half an hour, we were all getting into Mum's car, with Trenton at the wheel. My stomach was flopping about like a boat on a choppy sea.

We got to Barkingside and Trenton found a parking space miles up the road from Amarjit's flat. As we walked back towards it I saw the Vitara. I would recognise it a mile off, I knew it was Arun's. My heart was sinking. He had told me that his dad was not a man to go back on his word. So how had he managed to get the motor?

The party was in full swing as we stepped into the hallway. People started to greet Trenton and Zara and I just tagged along behind. I wanted to remain in the background, because if possible I wanted to observe Arun without him knowing that I was there.

Then I spied him.

He was talking to a guy and a girl and he had a drink in his hand.

The guy finally walked off, leaving him with the girl. Was she the one that he had passed me over for? She was looking into his face like a lovesick animal. I wanted there and then to claw her eyes out. Another guy came up and put his arms around the girl. I could see that she didn't like it, but she didn't push him off. They chatted for

155

a bit and then Arun turned and walked off.

My eyes were following him as he paused to talk to another girl. Then he made his way towards the door and me. He hadn't clocked me yet, but my heart started to pump up the volume like the background music of a thriller movie. He stopped just before the door to let someone come in and he turned his head. Our eyes locked.

My heart was in overdrive. It was weird. Just like you read about in books or see on the telly. Time really stood still. It sounds soppy and predictable, but it was as though no one else was in the room. We were alone. A lump came to my throat and it made breathing hard.

'Is this love?' I thought to myself. It felt painful and tight. I couldn't tell whether it was a good feeling or bad.

Arun came and stood next to me. 'What are you doing here?'

Without looking at him, I said, 'The same thing you are.'

He sipped his drink. I could tell he was embarrassed. Good.

'Come outside, I want to talk to you.' I didn't want to go.

Just then Priya bounded up to us. 'Hi, you two love-birds.' The beaming smile that she had on her face fell off as she looked at me. 'Eh, see you both later.'

Reluctantly, I went outside with Arun. He led me to the Vitara.

'How come you're driving?'

He didn't answer. We clambered into the car.

'Hello? Can you hear me?' I waved at him.

He turned and looked at me. For a split second I thought he was going to say 'It's over' and panic hit me.

I looked out the window, trying to hold on to my sanity.

'Rell . . .'

I didn't turn to him, but whispered, 'Yes.'

'I should have told you about the party, shouldn't I?'

I shrugged.

'It was stupid of me. I wasn't thinking straight. I knew that Priya and Trenton would be coming and that you would probably find out. It was just that I wanted to come, but I couldn't face taking the bus.'

'Really? So what did you do, or should I say, what did you say, to get these wheels back?'

I knew what was coming.

It came.

'I, eh, eh . . .'

'What?'

I could have said it for him but I wasn't going to make his life easier. Besides, I could feel something stirring up in me, from the pit of my stomach. It wasn't good.

'Well. The truth is, I said that we had sort of finished.'

'You lied. Or is it true and you haven't told me yet?'

'No, it's not true that we've finished, and I don't want us to be finished.' It all came out in a rush. 'Rell, you won't be able to understand what I'm going through. I've tried to explain it to you, but I don't seem to be able to get my words right. I've always had money, a car, all that sort of thing, and then to see them around me and yet not be able to use them is torture.'

'And so you lied.'

Mutely he nodded.

'Believe me, I didn't want to, but each day was getting harder. It's a trek and a half to the bus stop from my house

157

and if it wasn't for my brother slipping me some money, I really would be stuck.'

'And that's how you justify yourself!' I shouted at him. 'I've been through hell because of you, I've sacrificed a lot, and because you can't give up your creature comforts you resort to lies and deceit!' I felt really crazy. It was so hurtful to know that Arun had lied to his parents and was going to lie to me, if I hadn't found out about the party. 'What about afterwards? We would have to be sneaking around hiding again, I can't go back to that. You could have tried being more truthful. Maybe your parents would have come round.'

'No way, my dad's as hard as nails.'

'So, tell me something, where does that leave me, eh? Where does that leave us?'

He had to think.

I couldn't stand it any more. 'Take me home.'

Outside our house, we continued to thrash out our differences. The Vitara has central locking and it was only when I threatened to smash a window that Arun let me out. Half-running into the house I went straight to my room and threw myself down on the bed.

I didn't know if this was worse than him having another girl. He had been lying to me anyway. But then I thought, come on, you'd be devastated. Maybe I'm overreacting to this whole thing. But I felt so mad! Was I overreacting or wasn't I? Would I *ever* sort this out in my head?

★

I wanted to laugh. Aunt Melda had two big wads of cotton wool stuffed in her ears.

'Chile, when de plane lift off, me can't stand de popping in me ears.'

But as the plane became airborne, I found myself doing the same thing.

I closed my eyes. At last I was at peace with myself. I thought back to that night when Arun dropped me home and I felt grateful for what had happened. In the cold light of dawn, it had helped me to get things into perspective.

Mum had heard me crying and came into my room. I told her what had happened. She didn't seem surprised, and if she was pleased she didn't show it. All she said was, 'It's part of life, Rell, just put it down to growing pains.'

That night, I had finally reached a decision about me and Arun. It was time for us to split up – not because it was the easy answer, but because I'd lost faith in him. He had never really stood up to his parents, he had lied to them and to me, and I couldn't pretend these things hadn't happened. I didn't regret going out with him – we had had some great times together, and I was glad I'd stood up for myself when it all got tough.

Would I go out with another Asian boy again? Well, next time I'd know what I was letting myself in for. Our cultures are very different and that can be harder than you might think. Our families and our friends might cause problems – even to the point of cutting us off. Complete strangers might stare at us and hassle us in the street. But I remembered that day with the skinheads, and those racist white people in the restaurant that night. When the chips were down, Arun and I were both up against the same kind of problems and it seemed daft for us to be forced apart.

I hadn't changed my mind about all mixed-race relationships. I liked Zara a lot now, and if she and Trent were happy, I was happy for them too. But when Trent decided to ask Zara out, I'll bet he was thinking how good it would be for his image to have a blonde, blue-eyed girl on his arm and I don't think that attitude does anyone any good. But as far as Arun and I were concerned, at the end of the day, we'd split up because we weren't right for each other, not because black people and Asian people couldn't be together.

For the first few days afterwards I didn't want to talk to Arun, but then I thought that that was silly.

So we spoke, and arranged to meet in the park that afternoon.

Even though it was hard, I told him it was best that we were just good friends. He didn't want that. He wanted to be my boyfriend and he told me that he was willing to tell his parents the truth.

'Listen, Rell, I can easily get a part-time job, until I go to college. Don't let's finish. We can make a go of it.'

He was probably right, we could make a go of it, but I didn't want to. Not now. Finally I managed to convince him I meant what I said.

He looked really upset. 'I'm going to miss you, Rell,' he whispered. He quickly kissed me on the cheek, then turned and walked away.

The plane cut through pockets of fluffy clouds as it made its way to Florida. I didn't want to think about Arun while I was there. And I didn't want to get involved with anyone else, regardless of what Mum says.

I just wanted to get on with the rest of my life – to be me and have a good time!

grab a livewire!

real life, real issues, real books, real bite

Rebellion, rows, love and sex . . . pushy boyfriends, fussy parents, infuriating brothers and pests of sisters . . . body image, trust, fear and hope . . . homelessness, bereavement, friends and foes . . . raves and parties, teachers and bullies . . . identity, culture clash, tension and fun . . . abuse, alcoholism, cults and survival . . . fat thighs, hairy legs, hassle and angst . . . music, black issues, media and politics . . . animal rights, environment, veggies and travel . . . taking risks, standing up, shouting loud and breaking out . . .

. . . grab a Livewire!

For a free copy of our latest catalogue,
send a stamped addressed envelope to:

The Sales Department
Livewire Books
The Women's Press Ltd
34 Great Sutton Street
London EC1V 0DX
Tel: 0171 251 3007
Fax: 0171 608 1938

Also of interest:

Millie Murray
Cairo Hughes

Cairo Hughes is 16, adopted and loves her family. There's just one
problem. She's black and they're not.

Even though she knows they love her too, Cairo often feels like
she doesn't belong. Then her family move to London and, for the
first time, Cairo gets to know other black people. Her new friend
Diane is cool, confident and proud – and she has a gorgeous
brother, Reece. With Diane's encouragement, Cairo discovers an
exciting new world. But Cairo also realises that she needs to
understand her own heritage to be true to herself – even if it
means hurting those she cares about most ...

Fiction £3.50
ISBN 0 7043 4936 1

Millie Murray
Kiesha

**'Kiesha! Kiesha! Turn that music down! What are you doing
up there, having a disco?'**

Finding the space to do your own thing isn't easy. But Kiesha's
determined. She dances with Prince and Michael Jackson in her
bedroom; experiments with new hairstyles; and works *hard* at
getting her parents back together.

But now Mama Tiny is moving in and although Kiesha loves her
grandmother, losing her own bedroom is going to be hard. Even
worse, it's beginning to look like Kiesha's dad has gone for good . . .

'Immediate, accessible, warm and honest . . . A must.'
NATE News

Fiction £3.99
ISBN 0 7043 4129 8

Millie Murray
Lady A – A Teenage DJ

'Lady A just wants to say I've gotta go, But don't go away,
Stay with Radio Ess Jay Aay . . .'

August lives with her mum, her stepdad and her younger brother,
Troy. Her mum criticises her all the time, her stepdad doesn't
know how to handle her and she wishes she had as much
confidence as her wild best friend, Fleur. She can't remember her
real dad, and longs to meet him. Then August goes for a weekend
job on her local radio station. And when she gets her own
programme, things really start to look up . . .

'Riotous and down-to-earth.' *Africa World Review*

Fiction £2.95
ISBN 0 7043 4920 5

grab a livewire!
save £££s!!! with this voucher

Buy any of the following books and get
£1 off each book you buy! Post-free!

save £££s with this voucher!

Cairo Hughes by Millie Murray

Kiesha by Millie Murray

Lady A — A Teenage DJ by Millie Murray

Between You & Me: Real-life Diaries and Letters by Women Writers edited by Charlotte Cole

Name _____

Address _____

       '   _____

         _____

Postcode _____

I would like:

——— copies of **Cairo Hughes** at £3.50 less £1 = £2.50

——— copies of **Kiesha** at £3.99 less £1 = £2.99

——— copies of **Lady A — A Teenage DJ** at £2.95 less £1 = £1.95

——— copies of **Between You and Me** at £4.99 less £1 = £3.99

——— Livewire catalogue

Total enclosed £ _____

Do not send cash through the post. Send postal orders (from the Post Office)
in pounds sterling or cheques made out to The Women's Press.

Send this form and your cheque or postal order to The Women's Press,
34 Great Sutton Street, London EC1V 0DX. Allow up to 28 days for delivery.
Do remember to fill in your name and address!

This offer applies only in the UK to the books listed above, subject to availability.
This voucher cannot be exchanged for cash. Cash value 0.0001p